American Snowflake

A Hollywood Liberal's Journey from Democrat to Republican.

I0628413

By

ROMAN DRAKE

Table of Contents

Election Day, San Francisco, November 4, 2008

It was a chilly San Francisco night that was filled with people standing shoulder to shoulder. The joy was incredible. People were climbing street poles and cheering, and strangers were hugging and crying. Everyone had spontaneously left their apartments to celebrate with each other the hope that was coming to America. It was a great time to be alive and to know that, finally, change was coming. I stood there and closed my eyes in the middle of San Francisco, and I did something I hadn't done since my childhood in Indiana, which would normally feel inconsequential but felt appropriate in a time like this—pray.

I know, right? It's weird to admit, but it's a truth I never told anyone until now. I stood there in Pacific Heights, San Francisco, and prayed the war in the Middle East that killed thousands of innocent lives would soon be over. I prayed that the recession that was put upon us by the greed of the wealthy would soon be over too. I also prayed that the corrupt and evil Bush administration would leave quickly and peacefully. I opened my eyes and was relieved that I only had two more years before I graduated from my San Francisco Art School; it couldn't come fast enough. It was time to change America for the better just as Obama was about to. Los Angeles was waiting for me, and I couldn't get out of San Francisco fast enough.

Hollywood Hills, 2012

Everyone sat around in colorful leather bean bag chairs in the living room of an enormous Hollywood Hills house with exorbitantly priced art on the walls. Odd middle-eastern music played in the background. I wore a Fidel Castro T-shirt with a blue velvet suit jacket. I had spent most of the party talking about the new book I was writing called *American Slave*. I wrote a fictional story comparing the lives of minimum wage employees to slaves of the 1800s.

We all sat down and started listening to another author who was African American with dreadlocks. He had gold teeth and wore platinum chains, and he was speaking about systemic oppression, which was a term I had never heard of before. As I sat there and listened, it sounded like every law that was ever created in America was racist. Every law seemed racist, because the people at the time who created the laws also owned slaves. As I sat there in my Castro T-shirt, with two-hundred-dollar blue velvet suit jacket, I thought: *That's an odd belief to have.* The room was full of peer writers, filmmakers, musicians, who all sat there and nodded their heads in agreement to this. He was walking around the room, talking loudly, and pointing his finger at us. He said, "White people are responsible for enslaving Black people to this *very day*! White people uphold the laws that were created by their ancestors! White people *are* responsible for slavery!"

I was kind of confused. I looked around the room and kept waiting for someone to say something, but no one did. I thought, *Screw it.* Finally I blurted out, "Excuse me, but wouldn't that mean freedom of speech is racist too?" The Black author stopped in his tracks, almost like he had never been challenged before. I looked around and knew that none of these trust-fund children had ever lived in the parts of cities I had. They had never taken a wrong exit off the 110 freeway before. The author looked at me not knowing what to say. He quickly got angry and pounded his chest, "Each law was created by racists, for racists!"

I was genuinely confused. "So then your freedom to tell me this is...racist?" I asked, waiting for people to ask the same question I had. Again he seemed startled, looking around the room, not knowing what to say. "Black people are shot every day in this country! They are shot in the streets like Trayvon Martin was!"

Sitting there I was still perplexed, "Wait a second, wasn't Trayvon Martin shot in self-defense?"

"Trayvon Martin was shot by a white man for no other reason than being Black!" he said.

"That's not true. The shooter wasn't white; he was Hispanic. And *no*, he was not shot because he was Black!" I stated.

"He will never see justice because of people like you who prop up a system that puts Blacks in jail!" he stated.

At this point, I didn't know what to think. Everything he was saying was so beyond bizarre. "Black people don't go to jail because they are Black, they go to jail *if* they commit a crime," I retorted.

The blonde young woman who happened to be sitting next to me looked at me like she just saw a ghost. "Oh my God! Is he racist?!" she asked the room.

The Black author quickly pointed his finger in my face. "Yes! What we have here is a racist amongst us!"

All the white women in the room gasped. I frowned and scoffed, "That is ridiculous! The last thing on earth I am is racist." I looked over, expecting everyone to defend me, but they seemed to be mad—not at him but at me! They all had these angry-looking, disgusted mugs staring at me that seemed to say: *How dare you question someone with a darker shade of skin color than you!*

It was very strange to see. I was asked to leave the party by the young blonde woman from Hollywood Hills, whose father owned the house. She slammed the double doors on me as I left. As I walked down the long road, out of the gated community with a security guard, I tried to analyze what I might have said that was wrong. *How was I racist?* I got into my old, beat-up Volvo that stood out like a sore thumb in Hollywood. As I started my car, I saw my copy of Karl Marx's *Communist Manifesto* sitting in the passenger seat. I looked at it and thought, *What really needs to happen is socialism.* That Black author's confused beliefs about racism will suddenly end if he just has free healthcare, housing, food, and money given to him per month instead of being forced to work. Real freedom will be when every citizen of America doesn't have to compete with each other for the pay of greedy corporations. I pulled my car out of the driveway and was convinced that socialism was the answer to everyone's problems, including my own.

Unfortunately though, a few months later, I found out that the angry author would never be able to partake in my idea of a perfect society. He was arrested for traveling with three pounds of marijuana and two AK47s over state lines. One of the rich white women in the room that night was arrested with him. She was sitting in the back of the room with curly brunette hair and thick Coke bottle glasses; she was irate when I dared to suggest that Black people don't get arrested based on their race. Apparently, it was a very racist thing to suggest.

February 2016, Bernie Sanders

I had not really paid much attention to politics over the last four years—in all honesty, it was since I voted for Obama in 2008. Yahoo News, HuffPost, and the *LA Times* reported how Obama was the best president to ever live, so there wasn't much to worry about during those years. I was inspired by the Occupy Wall Street movement in 2012. The 99% of the population was finally ready to fight back against the oppressive 1% who owned all the wealth. People were finally waking up to the evils of capitalism that I learned about from CNN and Huffington Post during the recession of 2008.

In 2014 I was down on my luck working at a non-artistic civilian job, when I was told I had to buy health insurance or pay a fine. My face scrunched up as I tried to make sense of it. It wasn't really the hope and change I imagined when I celebrated in that spontaneous city-wide election party for Obama in San Francisco several years ago.

In February 2016, I kept hearing the name Bernie Sanders on the radio. I wasn't intending to vote at the time, but I kept hearing his name so I decided to Google him. Bernie Sanders was a socialist just like me, and he wanted to give people free healthcare and free college. I was so excited and happy that I literally shook my fist in the air. It was just a matter of time before the government would give everyone money, and no one would ever have to work at an evil corporation unless they chose to again. The other 99% of the population would finally have real freedom; things were *finally* going to change. The conservatives' time in the spotlight was over, and everyone had woken up to the fact that we were all just slaves working for the rich, like I had written and hypothesized about in my 2013 book *American Slave*.

About a week later I bought a Bernie Sanders shirt online that read "Fucking Bernie Sanders!" I wore it around to all the bars in Belmont Shore, where I would go drinking with my friend Brian; he was originally from Indiana like I was and happened to move to LA the same year I did. We frequented the posh Belmont Shore bars on weekends, and people would stop me and say they loved my shirt. People would high five me as I walked past them. I specifically wore the T-shirt when Brian and I went out because he was a conservative, and he needed to wake up from all the "America is great" lies and consider supporting Bernie Sanders like I did. I was happy and 100% confident that America would soon be the socialist country I always dreamt of. It would take time, of course, as all things did, but Bernie Sanders would be the *real* change that Obama never was. People at bars continued to high five me and some even bought me a drink when they saw my Bernie Sanders shirt. I'm definitely for free tequila. My friend Brian, who grew up in a conservative Indiana family, was the only person in Los Angeles County who ever scoffed at my T-shirt. I didn't care, because he knew nothing about politics.

I have liberal–socialist views, obtained a master's degree, and wrote a book about the evils of wage slavery. I had optioned screenplays, and many, many Hollywood agents told me I was a genius. I was outraged when he told me that his mother and father who were both doctors; thought Bernie Sanders was crazy. "What?! Why?! America is the richest country in the world!" I told him.

I was raving mad. Brian went back to drinking his Guinness and smoking his American Spirit cigarettes, and he abruptly changed the subject. It was odd how he always seemed to change the subject when I brought up politics. I assumed his family and he were greedy people who didn't want to be fairly taxed to make things equal in America, which—to a decent liberal–socialist person like myself— is inexcusable and should be punishable by jail. But whatever, I loved Brian and his family despite our different backgrounds. Brian would hopefully see the light someday after I showed it to him, and then he'd share the truth with his family.

I wanted to teach Brian all that I knew, but it would probably be hard for him to understand. Rich people only got rich because of years and years of generational wealth from their family or because they cheated someone. Luckily, more people are beginning to know that now. But it's harder for some people to understand, because most people are very brainwashed in America; they aren't as aware of society as I am. The TV and film industry is on the same page as me too. People like Bill Maher and Michael Moore are icons who have helped shift America in the right direction. Liberal thinkers walk a very noble path, because they try to do what's good for the people first. Conservatives, like my friend Brian, should drink their Guinness, sit back, and let the more knowledgeable take over, for the sake of humanity.

A few months had passed, and it was now April; Bernie was in a tight race with Hillary Clinton. I wasn't worried at all. Hillary Clinton was some old corrupt bitch who was taken to the shitter by Barack Obama years ago. We didn't need to rehash her plunder of Haiti; her private server drama; her 30-year span in politics where 48 people from her inner circle were found dead; or her Clinton Foundation that had billionaires giving her money for favors. That was all old news and I was very confident—so confident that I bought a few more Bernie Sanders shirts. I voted in the primary for the first time since 2008. I happily declared on Facebook that I voted for the guy who flew coach. It was widely known that Bernie Sanders refused to sit in first class. He also refused to take money from big corporations. He was my hero, because he was a person who only wants to give all the help he can.

But Then Bernie Sanders Loses.

Bernie Sanders lost. "He lost?!" I blurted out loud in my hybrid. I pulled my car over on the Los Angeles 10 freeway. I yelled at the radio again. "He lost?!" I got home that evening, overate, drank myself in a stupor, and then stumbled to the bathroom of my house to throw up. I could barely stand. I was so mad that I drunkenly even decided to stop recording all of my favorite television shows like *Total Divas* from the E channel. I was oppressed by evil America once again!

I coincidentally was driving to Las Vegas that same weekend to party and gamble, but before I left all I could think about was the rich billionaires who gambled away their money there. I was oppressed by these filthy rich billionaires who ruined my life every day, and they had the gall to gamble it away! Soon Friday arrived and it was a typical sunny and beautiful California day, but for me it wasn't sunny at all. I was boiling over. There were poor starving people ravished by the ills of capitalism, and—of all people—*Hillary Clinton* won the primary just days before. I threw my luggage into the trunk of my car, as my Chinese–Cambodian girlfriend Hong yelled at me to stop. "Bad boy! I told you! Stop!"

Bernie had just lost, and to make things worse, my brand-new hybrid was oppressing me as well. I sat in the driver's seat, tried to turn the key in my car, but the engine wouldn't turn over. It was a bullshit greedy world when rich corporations intentionally make your new car battery die just so you have to buy another one. I opened the car hood, looked at my car battery, and thought how unfortunate it was that I was too smart to know how to change it. People who have master' s degrees and write books like I do have far too many superior ideas in our heads to know how to change car batteries. There isn't enough room in our brains for meaningless garbage like mechanical stuff; that's the kind of ignorant stuff that only conservatives know how to do.

One of my neighbors was able to jumpstart my car so that I could drive to the local auto parts store. Surely after I bought a new car battery, some poor misfortunate worker at the front desk would be there and know how to install it. I gave my one hundred and twenty dollars to the poor slave at the front desk; he probably wasted his entire life learning how to fix cars. Under my car seat was my ten-grand money roll of cash that I had mostly saved from screenplay rewrite jobs to gamble in Vegas. But now this evil corporation was dipping into that money to scam me on this car battery. I just knew these car companies probably get kickbacks to make parts on their cars fail faster. To make things worse and more outrageous, this poor cashier, who probably only cared about money, wouldn't put the car battery in for me when I asked. He said it was against store policy. *This capitalist society is crumbling everywhere.* Bernie Sanders loses and now this! Was I living in some kind of third-world country?! How dare he *not* put the car battery in for me!

This wasn't his fault though, he was simply a victim of our cruel society, just like me. But then—*eureka!*—I had an idea. Since we do live in an oppressive capitalist system, and he was just a poor wage slave who has been taught to only care about money and not the well-being of others, I could offer him twenty dollars to do the job. Of course he said yes. I watched him put in the car battery as I stood in the shade from the hot sun. I wondered if this poor guy even knew he was a slave to our capitalist system. I thought about how horrible it was that people didn't do anything for anyone unless someone offered them money, but I knew it wasn't this worker's fault. He probably wasn't smart enough to have a master's degree in fine arts like I did. *Life in America is such a tragedy*, I thought, as my one-hundred-and-twenty-dollar car battery was placed into my hybrid for me.

I pondered this horrible tragedy with my arms open under the blue sky, as I looked into the clouds. But then, he suddenly had the audacity to ask *me* for help. "Uh, sure," I told him. He asked me to hold on to the wrench. Could he not see my outfit? I had on a ninety-dollar pair of jeans. *What was happening to this country?! This is fucking ridiculous.* Bernie lost, my hybrid needed a new battery, I was going to Vegas with *only* 10k in cash to gamble, and now my hands and possibly even my jeans and car were going to get dirty. *America and capitalism must be stopped at all costs!*

Of course I couldn't tell this poor slave to the system that I couldn't hold his tool. It wasn't his fault that he needed help. I held on to the tool with my fingertips as he finished the job. He proclaimed, "All done!" like he had just achieved something great. I thought about teaching this ill-informed person a lesson in doing things for others out of kindness by not giving him the twenty dollars I had offered him. But I decided against it as he probably had kids, so I gave him his money anyway. I got into my hybrid and was so pissed off that my eyes felt like they were bulging out of my head. I had dirty hands that were about to make my steering wheel filthy. There was absolutely no way I was going to use an auto store bathroom, so I drove across the parking lot to a classy little bar I frequented. I had spent hundreds of dollars there per night on weekends, so I knew they wouldn't mind if I used the bathroom.

The chic bar had a more pristine bathroom. I walked in and greeted a few drunks I knew and the bartender I've talked to probably three or four times. I walked past them all and went into the bathroom to wash my hands. After my hands were clean, I thought, *Perfect! All is well again.* I came out of the bathroom smiling, ready to go pick up Hong and drive to Las Vegas. But then as I was passing the bartender, about to leave, out of nowhere the bartender yelled at me, "Hey! You can't just come in here without buying something and use the restroom!"

I stopped in my tracks and turned my head ever so slightly. "Excuse me?" I asked. I must have misheard her considering I've been to this bar before and had spent literally hundreds of dollars there. She repeated herself, "I saaiiid, you just can't come in here and use the bathroom like that without spending money."

I couldn't believe it. I was floored. I walked up to the bar and pointed at her. "I have come into this bar and spent plenty of money. I even know the owner of the bar!"

The bartender responded, "I don't give a shit. You have to pay to use the restroom here."

I threw up my hands; I couldn't take it. The capitalism in this world was ruining all human decency. The anger in my head was at an all-time high. It was so hard to walk away from this but I wanted to try since she was just a brainwashed wage slave who had to work for a living. She didn't know any better. I tried to turn away from her. It took everything I had; I did it very slowly. But then in an instant, as I began to shake with anger, I flipped back around and proclaimed, "I'll never fucking come in here again!"

I showed her, I thought as I walked away, but then the bartender had the gall to apologize. "Umm sorry, sir, but rules are rules," she said.

I stopped on a dime. I turned back around. I could have crushed a tennis ball with my hand if I was holding one. I yelled, "No! Fuck that! Fuck everything!" I walked to my hybrid in the parking lot steaming mad, as everything bubbled to the top like water being boiled on a stove. I got in my car and drove home so raging mad that

I pounded my steering wheel with my fist. Over and over again I pounded the steering wheel. I pulled up beside my house to pick up my sweet girlfriend Hong, who wasn't aware of the cruel American world we lived in. For some reason she immigrated here from her socialist Cambodian country to this. "Everything okay, Daddy?" she asked as she sat in the passenger seat.

I looked at her happy demeanor, and her obliviousness to the evil American world. She always seemed happy and jovial, and I always wondered why. I had no idea how anyone in such a cruel capitalist world like this could ever be happy, but it made me glad that she always was. Just by looking at her smile, I suddenly felt calm. *Not knowing the truth must be bliss for her.* That's why I loved her. She could smile and be happy and not let the cruel American world get her down. It truly was a burden being as smart as I am, and I'm glad others don't have to bear that burden. I didn't want to ruin her innocence by waking her up to the evils of America. It was best she didn't know, and I didn't tell her. She sat there smiling at me, waiting for an answer to her question. "Yes. Yes! Everything is perfect!" I answered.

She shut the passenger door, and off we drove to Vegas. However, on the long five-hour ride there, as I helped her with her English along the way, the thoughts began to creep back about how horrible it was that Bernie Sanders lost. I couldn't stop thinking about how ridiculous it was that a city like Las Vegas existed while so many people were forced to work for a living at a job, sometimes eight to twelve hours a day. So when I got to my first baccarat table at Caesars Palace, I placed two hundred dollars on banker just for all the poor wage slaves in America who were forced to work. You'll never guess what happened—the banker turned seven. It was a dragon. I had placed twenty-five dollars on the dragon bonus and just won one thousand dollars, plus the two hundred I put on banker. Hong grabbed my face and kissed me. "My good boy!" she said.

All of the old Asian baccarat players came over to see me and pat me on the back. *I should give this money to charity*, I thought. But no, if I did that, some evil corporation might pocket it and use it for themselves. It will go to better use if I keep gambling and start putting double the money on dragon.

The DNC Convention

I still had hope. Bernie hadn't bowed out yet. Out of all the people who crossed my path while working in Hollywood, there wasn't one person I knew who voted for Hillary Clinton in the primaries. I was convinced something was up. Knowing Hillary Clinton and her history, it wasn't a giant leap to make. The FBI was currently investigating her and her phony Clinton Foundation. The scandals she was involved in included Benghazi; her illegal private server; her emails; smashing cell phones that the FBI requested; lying under oath; destabilizing the Middle East with horrible foreign policy as Secretary of State; and let's not forget the 48 people who suddenly wound up dead in her immediate circle over the last thirty years. I could go on and on, but it's too depressing to even think about.

Out of all the things Hillary had done and were widely known about, how could they let her go? It would seem that this would be the most important time to prosecute someone, especially since she was running for president—the most important job in the country—if she won. The Republicans had no chance.

But I was wrong; I couldn't believe it. This tall FBI agent, James Comey, strolled up on the TV and said Hillary was free to go. *What in the fuck is going on?* This wasn't the "great" American justice system I was taught about growing up. A little later news came out about a woman named Loretta Lynch, the attorney general to the Obama administration, who met with Hillary's husband Bill Clinton on a tarmac. This happened before the FBI came out and said that they weren't pursuing prosecution any longer. That sounds about right with everything we already knew about Hillary. I wonder how many bags of cash Lorretta Lynch received. Now suddenly after all the excuses they had for all the corruption that surrounded them, we were supposed to believe that Bill Clinton and Loretta Lynch only talked about grandchildren, golf, and traveling on that tarmac before exoneration from the FBI. *Really?* And what about everything else? Was Haiti just bad planning? It was all the more reason not to vote for her then. And what about the cattle's future controversy? Was it just lucky trading? Why did she have her intern's phones smashed?

On one *VICE News* episode on HBO, a father was reading his two daughters a children's book about how fantastic a woman Hillary Clinton was, and how she was going to break the glass ceiling for women and become president. I began to wonder if this was reality. The shady and corrupt shit this woman did could go on for a whole book—and in fact it did. There have been several books written about Hillary Clinton's corruption. Bill was the schmoozer and the one people liked, and Hillary was the gangster. I could understand one or two controversies and give her the benefit of the doubt, but it was harder to overlook around two hundred controversies. However the media and its celebrities had half the country already convinced. The news made it all seem like it was no big deal. I had *never* seen the drooling and fawning over someone who was as corrupt as Al Capone. Oh wait...yes, I did. But this guy didn't have any scandals. He was clean as a whistle. He was just about perfect in every way.

The last eight years the media did seem to fawn over Obama, but that was understandable because he was awesome. He never really did anything bad. He had zero scandals; at least I had never heard of any. I mean I didn't really pay attention in 2012 because he wasn't far enough left for me economically, but surely this wasn't the same thing as Obama. Obama was cool. All the news for eight years said he was the best president ever. But for some reason the Democrats had been put in a haze by Hillary Clinton. They had every excuse and talking point for everything. All of them were so confident that she was this terrific, innocent grandma. Then it came time for the DNC Convention. And at this point I was sure Bernie would still get the nomination. There was no way Hillary Clinton would be the nominee. *No way!* I watched patiently and was positive that my superhero Bernie Sanders would be the one who was selected, despite only speculation at this point that something was up with the primary. Surely people had to realize by now that we needed to stick it to the corporations, and not let Hillary Clinton dry hump them to death for eight years. Everyone was questioning the primary, except of course the DNC and the major news networks.

CNN said that Bernie Sanders was a sexist because he wouldn't bow out of the primaries. To Bernie's credit, he laughed at CNN when they reported that people said that. What an odd accusation for a news channel like CNN. I was now watching CNN more than I had in eight years, and some things were getting pretty strange over there, but whatever. I was too excited to see the protests outside the DNC. People were ready for *real* socialism! I was ecstatic when I realized this might actually happen; people were just as pissed off as I was. As the convention started, people inside began to walk out. But oddly, all the lights at the convention went out on camera. It was if they didn't want people to see it. But you could see it, clear as day, it was all the Bernie Sanders supporters. Then I saw a journalist on CNN who said that he wanted to get both perspectives, from the Bernie supporters and Hillary supporters. First we heard from this middle-aged, pissed-off feminist Hillary supporter. The young white male millennial waited on the other side of the journalist. The pissed-off Hillary supporter said, "As white people, we are privileged, and we need to think about other races."

"What?! What the fuck is this woman talking about?!" I asked the TV. "That didn't even make sense! What's the color of anyone's skin have to do with anything?" I blurted out loud. *But not to worry*, I thought, *this Bernie Sanders millennial is gonna mop the floor with her when the microphone goes to him.* The CNN journalist then turned to the camera, "Well it looks like we ran out of time. Back to you at the studio!"

"What?!" I screamed out loud at my TV. "He didn't even let the Bernie supporter say anything!" This middle-aged feminist cat lady Hillary supporter said something moronic about race, then this journalist fuck said he ran out of time before letting the Bernie supporter speak. *What was going on with these people?* This was beginning to get a little too obvious. Surely that was a coincidence, and they didn't mean for that to happen. It was almost like Hillary Clinton was in control of the DNC, and the DNC was in control of CNN and the rest of the media. Maybe this was all just a coincidence though. Surely they would say something else about the protests, because they wouldn't want to alienate half of the voting base who was seeing the same thing I was. The corporations and the one percent were stealing money and unfairly paying people low wages, and CNN put some crazy cat lady on to mammer about racism.

I saw plenty of coverage from conservative media on the Bernie Sanders protest, and of course it was understandable that they loved the division between these two factions. But it was like the protest didn't exist at CNN or anywhere else in mainstream media. It was beginning to become very clear to me that they were telling Bernie supporters to shut up and vote for who they told people to. With everything I knew about Hillary, I didn't even think it was possible to get to this point. I didn't think I'd ever have to vote for someone like Hillary Clinton in my life, because who in their right mind would actually let her get to the general election? She was facing Donald Trump, so of course she would win. Donald Trump was a joke and not even worth talking about; he only was a billionaire because he got his money from his dad. It was nepotism, and our country would be controlled by an oligarchy if that happened. The economy would crash under Republicans. Hillary Clinton was going to be president of the United States.

Then later into the night at the convention came Bernie's turn to endorse *her*—no way! Bernie has too much integrity; I mean, he even flew coach in airplanes instead of first class. Only true fighters for the people fly coach when they could fly first class. Bernie was the only person to understand how to fix this country. And then he stood up and took the microphone. I was positive that Hillary must have paid him off or threatened him with something and he caved to it. Why else would he endorse the devil?! This was a classic case of evil winning over good. This was what millennials like me didn't want in the world anymore; this was too much injustice for one night— Hillary supporters were jumping up and down because Hillary Clinton had a vagina and Bernie had a penis.

The DNC had its woman; the general election would be between a greedy and corrupt politician versus a greedy and corrupt businessman. But I'm supposed to vote for the greedy and corrupt politician because she's a woman and racism is bad? We all know racism is bad! In all my years of existence, I have never met a KKK member in all my life, and now I was told to vote for Hillary Clinton because, apparently, racists were everywhere? I didn't get it. Donald Trump would be the worst thing that could happen, but Hillary Clinton was a close second. And with the way they just shit on Bernie supporters at the DNC National Convention, it would take a miracle for them to pull off a vote from me.

This hysteria about racism and sexism reached points I have never seen before at the convention; that's what every speech was about. Why the hell were these people so out of touch and living in the past? Were these people watching too much *Mad Men*? What had happened to the people fighting for the average working citizen, regardless of race or gender? Apparently, they were nowhere to be found. When I looked at Donald Trump, I saw a rich, old dude who was handed everything from his father. I despised people like this, and in Los Angeles these people were all around. Their daddy started some million-dollar tech company in the nineties and now gave their kid a few million dollars to try to make it in the film business. People like Donald Trump got moved to the front of the line all the time, while regular hard-working people like me eeked it out just to get some rewrite jobs or a book published.

And if kids like Donald Trump aren't talented enough, it won't matter. Daddy will still pay for the piece-of-garbage script to get past all the gatekeepers. Donald Trump was the avatar for these kinds of people. They are super cocky, with no clue that they had it easy, and they have no problem telling everyone with a straight face that they worked hard. Donald Trump was the epitome of everything I hated. I wanted my superhero Bernie Sanders to tax the hell out of people like this. All these Hollywood Donald Trump rich kids would have to give their money to people like me, who had a lower- or middle-class upbringing, to make it equal. And a wall? I had no idea why Donald Trump was talking about a wall. CNN never said anything about immigration, or illegal immigration, so obviously it was *not* a problem. If it was a problem, CNN or one of the other TV channels or websites would have been reporting it, right? Fox News?!

Don't get me started on Fox News; it is made of conservative propaganda, evil, and lies. After all, CNN said that all the time, and CNN was a *real* news organization—except for all the race pimping and biased garbage they reported the last few months. That didn't make sense, but whatever. I started to wonder how a wall would help get the US citizens higher wages and better jobs from these rich evil corporations. I would rather mandatorily make small business owners pay twenty dollars an hour to their employees. They should be able to afford it, and if not, that's not my problem. Between mass hysteria race-pimping Hillary supporters versus the delusional America-loving Trump supporters, there weren't options at all for me. I tossed and turned a few nights as I knew I would not be voting in 2016.

But about a week later, I could finally sleep again. Soon after when I was on Facebook, confetti fell and doves flew into the sky when I saw the flower child that is Jill Stein. She was like some of the old hippie girlfriends I had in San Francisco. They were all around fifty-five, never married, no kids, three college degrees, and just as many cats. Of course once I saw Jill Stein's intense emotional campaign video about how we are all oppressed living under an oligarchy, I was sold. She also had some racial justice crap mixed in there but whatever; I could live with a small amount of that bullshit for the Black vote.

It's odd how politicians seem to lie to Black people just to get their vote. But whatever, I know no one on the left is truly racist. They talk about being not racist all the time, so of course they aren't. Just tax the rich already! I was one hundred percent for Jill Stein. She was a third-party candidate, but miracles can happen; I lived in Los Angeles and saw it every day when the lane opened up for me on the 210 freeway. As a liberal and economic socialist, every election was life or death. We must have unfettered access to government control, because peace, love, and smashing evil corporations who take advantage of people depend on it.

Four Months of the Circus

Everywhere you looked, everywhere you went, there was the election.

Either it was praise and glorification for Hillary Clinton or it was hatred and disgust of Donald Trump. All I heard every day was how great Hillary Clinton was or some absurd comparison of Donald Trump to Hitler. Although Hitler was a bit of an exaggeration, Trump would be far worse than George W. Bush, who was like the devil for me when I was going to college in San Francisco. I had been told so many times that Bush was Hitler that it was confusing to me because now they said Trump was Hitler. I had gone to many anti-Bush protests and even held signs saying Bush was Hitler. It was a given that Trump would crash the economy if elected. All economies need heavy regulation so that they can succeed, and Trump would do the opposite. *Thankfully that would never happen!*

The thick-skulled conservatives who built things and owned businesses just didn't know what was good for them. They should just lie down and accept the sweet embrace of Bernie's socialism. Something was wrong with them, but something was more wrong with these people dancing out in the middle of New York for Hillary Clinton on YouTube. They wore multi-colored pant suits, and all of their moves were choreographed to a dance song. Hundreds of them dancing in the middle of New York for a woman who took foreign money like she was the tooth fairy. Something about these artistic but delusional millennials dancing in the middle of New York for Hillary Clinton struck a chord in me.

After seeing this very cringeworthy music video for Hillary Clinton, the next YouTube video came on of the Berkeley University campus protesting the appearance of some guy named Ben Shapiro. They were burning cars, screaming about how he was a Nazi, and even invading his speech to chant something about racism. Who was this guy and why was Berkeley letting him speak if he was advocating violence on Black people? Were the Hillary supporters right—were we about to be living under Nazi control? I saw so many people who once lived in the same city with me destroying the campus of Berkeley. This guy must be an absolute monster to justify destroying your own property, right? *Right?!* I protested against George W. Bush in San Francisco several times, but never did I ever destroy my own stuff.

I needed to see who this guy was so I typed Ben Shapiro's name into YouTube. I clicked on the first video. It was Ben Shapiro explaining some kind of moronic bullshit about how socialism doesn't work. But the examples he used weren't *real* socialism. Russia had a dictator, and that's not the economic system of socialism. And then Shapiro said, "Facts don't care about your feelings." *Huh?* I played back the video. "Facts don't care about your feelings." He did kind of have a point. The author with dreadlocks at that Hollywood party years ago acted like he just got off the cotton plantation; he didn't provide facts about what he was talking about, but he had a ton of feelings about it.

Even though Ben Shapiro might be right about that guy, he was not right about socialism. The United States is the richest country in the world, so of course we should try socialism. I had never really looked into any of the facts or statistics either, but that was different, and I'm not good at math anyways. Plus Bernie Sanders said socialism was okay and so did the Democrats, plus all the movies I liked. All of Michael Moore's documentaries said socialism was good too. They wouldn't be so careless as to advocate for all this free stuff unless it was possible.

However, these were the same people who said to accept Hillary Clinton as our second mother and our liberal overlord, which was odd. But facts don't care about your feelings, and I *feel* that the facts *have* to be for socialism! Shapiro had one minuscule point about facts not caring about feelings that had absolutely *nothing* to do with me! I googled him. "Ha!" I said out loud. He was Jewish and wore a yamaka so of course he was not a Nazi or racist—dumbass, delusional Hillary supporters again.

I googled Shapiro further and found out he was a bourgeoisie millionaire's kid who grew up in Beverly Hills and went to UCLA. I would have to petition the universe if I'm ever reincarnated. I bet as soon as he came out of his mother's womb, a stockbroker was there to catch him and immediately asked what kind of stock options he would like to invest in. The American Dream is only for the few whose parents can afford it. *Whatever!* So Ben Shapiro had made *one* good point, although it didn't apply to me, but I doubted it would *ever* happen…again.

The Debate

This debate was hyped up to be a major heavyweight fight, and it was. The NFL was even claiming that TV ratings for football were down because everyone was so focused on politics, which seemed plausible because I was non-stop watching CNN every day. Who gave Don Lemon and Chris Cuomo a job? And did a Vanderbilt kid from Yale really need to be the lead host? About a week before the first debate, I began reading that Hillary Clinton had told her public relations people that it didn't matter who won the debate as long as the media told the public that *she* won the debate. She surely wasn't such a bad debater that she would lose to Donald Trump. She had essentially adopted all of Bernie Sanders' policies, and even though she was just using Bernie as a puppet to get to her throne, at least she was a Democrat and her policies would be better than Donald Trump's.

And then the time came. They strolled across the blue stage, shook hands, then both stood behind their own podium. Every answer from Hillary Clinton was packaged very well—shiny boxes of nothing with a ribbon tied to it. She said all the things people heard from every politician. And then there was Trump. I hated this guy. How was this reality TV host winning? He was decisive, had vision, was firm, and said what he really thought, and people could tell. He began attacking China right off the bat. I had never heard anything about China. *This was strange.* He said China was ripping us off on trade and stealing our jobs, so he was going to renegotiate our trade deals. I had never heard this stuff before. CNN had never talked about China.

Hillary Clinton's comeback was that she was going to invest in education. This was the same promise everyone had heard from politicians for the last sixty years. How does a politician fix anything when asked? Invest in education. How do they fix the economy? Invest in education. How do they fix bad trade deals? Invest in education. How do they fix anything and everything, according to a politician who doesn't really know anything but is looking to be elected? Invest in education.

And although Trump's behavior was aggressive, abrasive, and at many times funny, it looked like he was winning. I was always taught that you weren't supposed to treat women like he did. It was easy to see that Trump didn't care about the politically correct rules because his motivations were different. Hillary Clinton was there to be president of the United States and to be the center of virtue; Trump was there because he thought he could fix things. And this debate went on for two hours. Trump hilariously dug into her and dominating her—she appeared to be the fake politician we all saw her as. He told her that she had been fighting ISIS her entire adult life. It was an exaggeration but not much of one. I hated to admit it, but it was pretty funny. He torched her on her thirty-three thousand missing emails—again and again, with no mercy. Any other male candidate would have given her a break because she was a woman but not Donald. You could tell he was a scrapper. Donald Trump was the kind of guy who breaks his beer bottle to stab you in a bar fight. You could tell that Hillary was surprised and shaken. And then it was all over, and there wasn't much left of her. She was a beaten down old lady. Sure she had a few good jabs here or there, such as on his tax returns or his shady business dealings, but these were minor jabs that barely grazed the surface. He was a businessman. It was like saying a police officer likes doughnuts.

The Donald took her by her ankles, bounced her off the walls for two hours, and then threw her in a ditch. And what did the media say? Of course you know already; they said *she* won. They said *she* dominated *him*. They said *she* was the far better choice. This kindergarten teacher running to be president of the United States was supposedly going to end racism and sexism, which was something that really wasn't a major part of America anymore, by investing in education. This kindergarten teacher was going to bring back high paying jobs by investing in education. Over and over again, every problem of America was going to be fixed by some vague solution, like investing in education. Investing in education has been done in excess for years and years, but Hillary Clinton attempted to make it sound like a cool new idea. And we were all supposed to believe that *she* won? The media was all telling us to go along with it. We were all told to accept it and not even think about Donald Trump, because he was sexist and racist.

Trump had been in the public eye for around fifty years, and no one ever said he was racist or sexist then. He hung out with 2 Pac and

Mike Tyson, for Pete's sake! Many people of diverse races loved him. He was awarded over and over again by civil rights activists like Al Sharpton and Jesse Jackson. He was the reason golf courses in Florida were desegregated for Black people and Jewish people. But *whatever*—he was still a rich old guy who was given money from his daddy to make it. He would obviously never win, and thank God for that. The last thing I wanted was the economy to collapse. But then came the mainstream media's favorite news story of the century.

The Pussy Grabber

Why was this even news?! What do these moron Hillary supporters think is news?! They can't understand how young women might *let* a seventy-three-year-old famous billionaire grab their pussy? Well it certainly wasn't because of his looks! Bahaha...(gasp for air)...bahaha! Who are these people? Don't they remember Monica Lewinsky taking a cigar up her ass from Hillary Clinton's husband, Bill Clinton? Do we really have to explain to these people that some women like power, money, and fame? I live in Los Angeles, so give me a break already! If liberals had their own country, California would be it, and Los Angeles would be the capital. There was pussy being sold here up and down Sunset Boulevard for jobs in waitressing, and liberals suddenly couldn't understand how a woman might *let* a billionaire grab her pussy? Oh please, let's have a reality check! Los Angeles is a city of ten million liberals, and not one of them is an angel. I'm sorry, but I haven't met many liberal nuns who have come out to Los Angeles to be famous actresses. But sure enough, here they came. All the mad three hundred-pound feminists who couldn't get a date if their life depended on it were outraged that Donald Trump told the truth in a private conversation. How dare he do that!

The outrage grew, and of course everyone rushed to social media to say how horrible Donald Trump was and how they couldn't wait for Hillary Clinton to be president. That's all we heard. But of course Hillary had more skeletons in her closet than a dungeon master, and even a catastrophic mistake by Donald Trump would only last a few hours before she fucked up. It was just a matter of time before the media began covering for her like a covert American military operation gone wrong. Sure enough, on the same day, here it was. It was Donald Trump joking about women letting him grab their pussy because he's famous, versus Hillary Clinton explaining her idea for an open border, open market hemisphere, with shanty towns all around the United States. Wikileaks released all of her DNC emails. America is obsessed with degeneracy of course. So no, Hillary Clinton and her airheaded welcoming of open border destruction wasn't news. Having open borders with countries south of us, with crime three times the amount of crime in the US, wasn't news at all. Having open borders with people who worked for one dollar a day, or even less, wasn't news either.

CNN spent thirty seconds to two minutes on Hillary Clinton's Wikileaks and her idea for open borders, and they acted as if it was all just gravy. I watched one day as the CNN anchor Chris Cuomo even reported that we weren't allowed to look at Wikileaks, because it was against the law; we were only allowed to learn about Wikileaks through CNN. I stared at the TV, "Uhhh, suck my dick, Chris Cuomo." What we heard over and over again was, "Oh my God! How can we vote for this man to be president?! This disqualifies him! He can't be president!" One crazy person after another, from one news channel to the next, all said this in what seemed to be an attempt to outdo each other. There was massive hysteria on all news channels of the shocking revelation that women like money, fame, and power. Who would have thought?! This would go on for twenty minutes of a thirty-minute show, with three intervals of three-minute commercials, twenty-four hours a day, seven days a week.

But don't worry, CNN saved thirty seconds to tell us that Hillary Clinton's dream for America is no big deal. It was no big deal for the country to be invaded by people with crime three times higher than ours and who would work for one dollar a day. It's not a big deal or anything, so just shut the fuck up and keep listening to this billionaire who admits he's not a virgin. How dare he! The whole thing was a joke. It was like living in an episode of the *Twilight Zone*. What was going on with the media and the Democratic Party?

The Second and Third Debates

The second and third debates ended up much like the first: Hillary was torn apart, and Trump never missed one opportunity to kick her in the teeth while she was down. She was an easy target. She was the worst candidate ever. She was the most corrupt, two-faced, business-as-usual politician we had ever seen; however, the liberals didn't care because they wanted the first woman president. In unison, celebrities, media, and the Democratic Party said that women needed to be the ones to lead us into the future. It didn't make much sense but everyone was very eager to go along with it. I had spent my entire life picking men first in competitive sports, and now they were telling me I needed to pick a woman because she was stronger.

The media and the Democratic Party made excuse after excuse for this woman. They sent her off to be bombarded by the most ruthless machine gun-mouth America had ever seen. Donald Trump was a mixture of a standup comedian and a doctor getting straight to the point and telling you how disgusting and fat you are. I couldn't tell where the media began and the Democratic Party ended. And they sent a kindergarten teacher with more holes than Swiss cheese up against cannon gun-mouth Trump—it was absolute murder. If you turned on the TV after the debates, however, it was the most out-of-touch anchors you'd ever see, telling you that Hillary Clinton won by a landslide. Supposedly decimated Hillary had wiped the floor with Trump, and we were all supposed to believe it. The media rammed down our throats over and over again that Hillary Clinton was the best option.

These people were not just telling us what to think, they were demanding it. They expected it. After all, these news anchors, TV hosts, and famous personalities, were from prestigious, elite families who went to Ivy League schools. It would not only be rude if we didn't listen to them, it would be nearly a crime. CNN, MSNBC, ABC, CBS, and NBC all knew best. Listen to them and do what they say, because if you don't, America will collapse into a Nazi regime. Everyone was voting for Hillary Clinton. You don't want to be thought of as a freak, do you?! During one broadcast, when one CNN on-site correspondent began thoroughly discussing Hillary's Wikileaks scandal, she was suddenly cut off air. She came back on promptly and the subject was changed. CNN cut audio of one political consultant after another if any criticism of Hillary Clinton was ramped up a smidge past two on the volume level. In one instance a political analyst was cut short for daring to say he was voting third party.

These media games helped me quickly make up my mind—I was definitely voting for Jill Stein. It was very clear that people weren't allowed to disrespect the queen Hillary Clinton. Any conservative political consultant with a bit of a chip on their shoulder for Clinton, and the nonexistent Hillary criticism in the media, was immediately cut. They either came back with a completely different attitude or were not brought back at all. Chris Cuomo was heard saying, "Oh no, that sucks!" very sarcastically when one conservative political consultant was cut, after he brutally went about dismantling Hillary Clinton and her numerous corruption scandals. I had never seen anything like that in my life, at least not that I'm aware of.

But it was so bad, so obvious, that I immediately began to wonder. Did I not notice that the media was this biased for Obama all along? Had I been duped by the media that Obama was the best president of all time? *No way,* I told myself. I'm smarter than that. Obama implemented many changes like Obamacare that I was forced to pay for or be fined for not having. Okay, maybe that sucked. But there was no way the media needed to be biased for him like they had been so blatantly doing for Hillary Clinton. Obama's news coverage was so good that I lost interest and just checked out for eight years. *Surely that was all correct, right?* I pushed those thoughts away. This couldn't be anything but a corrupt Hillary Clinton who played puppeteer of the media. She had been in politics for thirty years, and her influence was everywhere: from LA, New York, to DC.

These TV anchors and newspaper/website journalists were doing backflips for her. I couldn't remember seeing them do that for Obama, or was it that I just didn't notice? I was a kid when my parents voted for Bill Clinton, but I would have definitely noticed then. *Right?!* I pushed those thoughts even further away. Donald Trump must *not* win, because our whole economy would collapse. Rich people would have more freedom to make all the money they want, and *that* would collapse the economy. I was also beginning to realize that Hillary Clinton must *not* win either. The derangement and delusional behavior on television were really starting to worry me. The economy was already anemic, and with Hillary Clinton it could very well collapse too. Although she was corrupt and careless, our country would be worse off under Trump, I was 100% positive of that. At least with Hillary she might have found time between hoarding foreign money and offing witnesses to at least bail out millennials and all this student debt. That would help cure this economy and put this evil capitalism in its place—at least until we could elect Bernie Sanders.

Hillarity Clinton – A Side of Beef Being Thrown in a Van

I had never seen a more manipulative politician than Hillary Clinton. After all of Clinton's lies by her and the media, after all the stories of corruption that the media did backflips to clean up after, people were served another giant whopper. It was in the form of a very nonsensical reply to Donald Trump's claim that Hillary Clinton didn't look healthy. A Hillary Clinton spokesperson came on TV to say that Hillary was in *perfect* health. The public was made to believe that Hillary Clinton was the healthiest American. The Hillary Clinton employee droned on about how strong and in perfect health she was. It had seemed just like an off-the-cuff comment by Donald Trump at one of his rallies. But now the Hillary team went berserk to make sure everyone in America thought of this old lady as the epitome of personal fitness and health. Hillary Clinton even went on a late-night TV show to open a jar of pickles. It was ridiculous, as if opening a jar of pickles on TV was a doctor administering a physical in front of everyone. The strangest part was that the jar of pickles didn't even pop. It was very obvious that the seal was previously opened, and Hillary only needed to open up the jar the rest of the way.

The media continued to make it seem like Hillary Clinton could run a 5k marathon. It was very obvious what the media wanted everyone to think of her, but at the same time, *why*? Yeah, she was an old lady, but what was the big deal? Why was there constant manipulation of what people should think? Why was the media continually trying to shape the way the public thought of Hillary's health? Since they were ramming down our throats how healthy Hillary Clinton was, well then, the opposite must be true. Everything else had been a lie up to this point, so this must be a lie too. She probably had cancer, AIDS, heart disease, and I wouldn't be surprised if she had Ebola too. Maybe the Clintons and their servants in the media were just overreacting. So maybe, just maybe, for the first time in all of this, there wasn't much to it. *Annnd* then she passed out on the side of the street. It was after a memorial service for 9/11, and while she walked up to the van she fainted right in front of everyone.

Her handlers attempted to stand her up. It looked like a scene from the movie *Weekend at Bernie's.* This woman was not only the biggest liar I had ever seen, but she was also the worst liar I had ever seen. The Internet, which was the only check to the media's unchecked bias, played the footage over and over again. It was Hillary Clinton falling down and her handlers struggling to keep her up in front of cameras. After all the talk of how healthy she was, and the constant manipulation to make people believe she was healthy, this was absolutely hilarious! I saw the footage over and over again. I was very confident now that the media and her robot Hillary supporters were going to admit their wrongs, and finally hold Hillary accountable for lying to people about her health. Then they defended her. *Again!* What the fuck was going on?!

The same spokesperson who came on all the news channels to say how healthy Hillary Clinton was, came back on to say that she was still totally healthy; she just forgot to mention she had pneumonia. *What?!* She had been on every news channel, every day for two weeks. Hillary Clinton even went on late-night TV to open an already opened jar of pickles and, during all of this, her team who had been funded one billion dollars to defeat Donald Trump, forgot to mention she had pneumonia?!

This was the same team of people who were doing backflips since her nomination to make everyone believe she was honest, which any rational person knew she wasn't. The Hillary supporters from news media, social media, Hollywood, and the low IQ people all across America very quickly learned all the talking points. At this point I couldn't take it. I was headed to dinner in North Hollywood, where a famous celebrity's kid was going to be. Her dad had a small role on *The Sopranos* for a number of seasons. She was an artist who did weird things like put her used tampon on a canvas and sold it. She was a Hillary supporter and a pain in the ass as a human being, but we ran in the same circles. We sat there, at this upscale restaurant, and of course politics came up as it was coming up everywhere. I stayed clear of this topic with these people the whole time, except for the people who were closest to me.

On and on this person went, who grew up in a five-million-dollar home. She went on and on about how horrible Trump was. That was what they always did; if someone brought up anything about Hillary, they came back with an onslaught of how horrible and racist Donald Trump was. On and on she went with how ridiculous it was that conservatives were making a big deal about Hillary Clinton falling. She spoke confidently at the round table, not thinking that anyone at the table would think differently than her. The secret that these avid Hillary supporters didn't know was that, even in Hollywood, there were a ton of us who weren't duped like she was. In fact I knew a few people at the table of twelve who for sure weren't.

So I played with my lime over my Diet Coke and tequila, poking holes into it with my cocktail straw. This woman's complete lack of understanding of how the world worked was agonizing. Again and again this woman talked so confidently about how racism and sexism were the number one problem in America. Then she began to talk about just who this problem was coming from, which was of course...white men. I kept looking at all the white men sitting around the table, and I felt happy I wasn't the one who had to shut her up, because surely one of these scrawny eighty-pound men would say something, right?

After about ten minutes, I did a quick refresh of the table from my drink, and saw these supposed men actually look on interested in what she was saying. They were paying attention to her. She was talking about some bullshit toxic masculinity (I had never heard of this), white privilege, and systemic racism. All of the terms were so pseudo-intellectual, and these idiots were nodding their heads. They all said they were liberals, but they were talking about redistributing wealth. I liked the sound of the last part, but this other mumbo jumbo was hot garbage, and I certainly didn't think we needed to redistribute wealth to Compton, simply because of a certain skin color there.

I did a good job staying out of it, but now she was talking about how oppressed women were by men. She then said that there was no biological difference between men and women. *Ok enough,* I thought. "Hmm," I very loudly said to the rest of the table that had been listening to this garbage quietly for thirty minutes. Everyone quickly looked. A writer's assistant who worked for me a few times quickly sipped water and looked away, as if it would make her disappear from the dinner. The eighty-pound "men" around me all stared at me wondering what I was doing. I wasn't sent a memo on the backwards ideas these people had the last eight years, so I spoke up.

The girl looked at me in almost disgust that I, a white man, dared to even hint at challenging her. With everyone looking at me I tamed my response and asked a question. "So, you can't think of one biological difference between men and women? Not even one?" I asked.

"All of that can be changed. If I'm blonde I can dye my hair black," she said confidently.

"So then does that make your biological hair color black?" I asked.

She looked around the table smugly. "It's okay, guys, Roland is from Indiana," she said. Everyone half smiled, giggled, and smirked to themselves.

"Yes, we were taught science there," I said.

"Uh, I think UCLA is a bit better than whatever the fuck art school you went to," she said smugly.

"Not if you don't understand I have a dick and you have a vagina," I said with a smile on my face.

A few gasped, and one girl's water fell over. Here came the "men" to stand up for her. This guy was a hack of a writer but we all had to pretend he was good. We did this because he won some science fiction award four years ago, from an organization that only gave it to him because his mother was vice president. His mother was one of those hoity-toity people around town, who went about sucking movie executives off for status. She wrote one screenplay thirty years ago. Her son was sitting at our table with black sunglasses on. He quite possibly had the gayest name I ever heard—Dory. "Hey, gender fluidity is a real thing," he said in a way that was trying to come off as intellectual.

"Gender what?" I asked. This was the first time I had heard of this as well. I shook my head as I knew I was in for a treat.

"See. You don't even know what we are talking about," he said.

"Yeah. It sounds horrible," I replied. A few people snickered as he stared them down.

"There are transgender people right now being harassed and beaten because of Donald Trump and his campaign. He's firing up people like *you* from your state, who *love* fascism," he retorted.

"Excuse me? Did you say fascism?" I asked.

"We've always lived in a fascist country; you do know that, don't you?" he asked. I looked around the table. Surely someone was going to break up this lunacy. Mostly everyone looked away. Some people stared at me with a mad look.

"Look, I'm no fan of America either, but you can't say America is a fascist country," I said. About two or three of the twelve people laughed out loud. They thought it was so hilarious that I thought we didn't live in a fascist country. "So Obama is the president of this fascist country we live in?" I asked.

"The president doesn't matter; the laws matter," Dory stated.

"You mean like the first amendment that says we have freedom of speech or the second amendment right to bear arms? Or is it the nineteenth amendment that allows women to vote? Which laws are you referring to that make it so we are living in a fascist country?" I asked.

"When you have people of color fearing for their lives every day, then yes, we live in a fascist country," he answered. I laughed again. *What the fuck was this guy talking about?* This guy lived in Brentwood. He doesn't have a colored person living within a hundred miles of him, but somehow, he was the expert and knew that people of color fear for their lives? But just as this insanity was happening, a Black woman named Jacquelyn I knew who worked at a prominent movie studio was walking past the table. Jacquelyn was smiling with not a care in the world as she always did and didn't seem to be paying attention to our embarrassing conversation. Jacquelyn was Jamaican, nonpolitical, not opinionated about much, and one of the happiest people you could ever meet. I envied her.

"Jacquelyn! Hold on a sec, can I borrow you?" I asked. Jacquelyn stopped over by the table, smiling at all of us.

"Sure, of course, what is it?" she answered.

"I'm sorry I have to ask you this. But do you fear for your life living as a Black woman in Venice Beach?" I asked. The question itself was a joke. Go to Venice Beach for five minutes, and the biggest problem you will face is street parking or mistaking a multi-millionaire for a bum, since that look was fashionable over there. The more downtrodden you looked, the cooler you were in Venice.

Jacquelyn looked around the table with curiosity and, in all seriousness, asked, "Fear of what?"

I was embarrassed to answer the absurd question, but I did anyway to prove a point. "Fear of white people killing you, as this genius says," I said, pointing to Dory.

She looked over at Dory and gave a goofy smile and giggled, "Nooo!" she answered.

"You see, moro-?!" I started to ask.

And before I could even finish calling him a moron, he stood up and dashed toward Jacquelyn very intensely. It was if this was a matter of saving mankind. "Why would you say that, Jacquelyn?!" Dory asked in an exasperated voice. My face didn't know what to make of this situation, as this idiot stood on the other side of Jacquelyn and was now clutching her arm. Jacquelyn drew back from him and looked scared and confused. "Do you know the amount of Black people killed every day in this country?" Dory asked. Jacquelyn looked around not knowing what to do. She looked scared and frightened that this group of people were all staring at her now. She was worried that she may have said the wrong thing. I was shocked. I hit the table with my fist in anger as the whole table shook, which startled all of the overly sensitive drama queens sitting there.

"Hey, asshole! Do you know the number?!" I asked. Finally this dumb fuck stopped staring at her and took a look at me, weighing two hundred and twenty-five pounds, which is like a Brock Lesnar for the arts scene in Hollywood. I could have broken his eighty-pound frame like a twig. I moved Jaqueline aside and got right in this piece of shit's face. "Jacquelyn has a better chance of getting struck by lightning than being killed by a hate crime. Take your propaganda and stick it up your ass before I do it for you!" I loudly retorted. Dory, the little pussy he was, sighed and acted normal again. It was if this discussion was all just a game for him.

"Calm down....this is a dinner," he said as he walked away from Jacquelyn and sat back down at his seat. He pretended it was all nothing and that it was I who was overreacting. He went back to eating his warm marinated olives like nothing even occurred. I was shaking.

"Is this calm enough for you?" I asked. I picked up a stuffed siracha shroom and flung it at him. It hit his sunglasses streaking siracha all the way down the lenses. The whole table gasped, and the whole restaurant and gallery went quiet and looked. "You are wearing sunglasses in a restaurant, at nighttime!" I said. Two security guards were called.

The hostess came over to me. "Leave! Now!" she demanded.

Dory stood up like I just spit on his tiara. "Do you even know who my mother is?!" he yelled at me. I began to let the security guards escort me out.

"Yeah! She blew me in Palm Springs once," I said. She didn't but we were alone together for an awfully long time at a party once. I knew it would drive him insane to always wonder. Dory let a heave of hot air out of his lungs like the pissed-off child he was.

"You'll never be signed by _____ (some creative agency he had no power over, and neither did his irrelevant mother)," he snapped. It's funny when people get angry in Los Angeles; it's a common thread of events. First, they remind you who they are, then they remind you who their family is. Then of course they threaten you. They tell you that you will never work at some company that they have no actual power over. Plenty of people buy into this, especially many newcomers to Hollywood. So did I at one time. It's as bogus as their Scientology beliefs. Yeah you can lose business contacts and friends, but who doesn't in Hollywood? It's all about not letting people walk on you here.

The idea that there was some kind of genocide on Black people was false BS. This guy got a boner from wanting to tell people about it though. The idea that masculinity was toxic was also false. The idea that we lived in a fascist country was false. The idea that all white people are born with money was false too. *What the fuck was going on here?!* And where was I when all this stuff became mainstream? It seemed to happen overnight.

I got on the Sunset Strip and began driving home as all these thoughts swirled around in my head. Did Los Angeles drop acid? Was I the only one in this city who hadn't lost my mind?! Because of this election, this city was suddenly unrecognizable. I cheered myself up knowing that Donald Trump would lose. Hillary Clinton would be an awfully corrupt president, but these people would be insane if Donald Trump ever won. Yes, the country would fall under the rule of Walmart, or possibly the highest bidder from Wall Street if Clinton won, but at least all these empty skulled rich kids would forget about this stuff. No real action would take place under Hillary Clinton. Her open borders idea scared me, but surely these morons weren't for open borders. You'd have to be a complete imbecile to be for open borders. Hillary Clinton would still be far better than Donald Trump as president. All of Hollywood would turn upside down if Trump won; thank God that was not going to happen.

The FBI Investigating Hillary Clinton Again!

I woke up on a Friday morning to a text from my friend Brian. He had sent me a meme of Hillary Clinton in a white Ford Bronco, driving on the 710 freeway. It was the infamous OJ Simpson LA police chase. Except Hillary Clinton was in the front seat instead of O.J. and she was hightailing it away from LAPD. I turned on the television and Hillary Clinton was under investigation *again* by the FBI. They found more emails from Hillary Clinton that she attempted to delete. Even more stunning was that they found the emails on her assistant's husband's computer, who also happened to be a child molesting ex house of representative. You've got to be kidding me! What the fuck is going on here—why can't this woman just be normal?!

Yes, Donald Trump was a weirdo too, but this woman was supposed to be some kind of liberal superhero. She was supposed to be some kind of shrine to all that was good. People danced for her in the middle of New York. People actually believed she would end sexism and racism if elected. Still, even with the FBI investigating Hillary Clinton, all the public heard was, "What about Donald Trump?" Over and *over* again. These people would vote for the devil if it rose up from the ground and ran for president against Donald Trump. In fact these people were sure that the devil would be a better president than Donald Trump. And why was this? Because just like every republican candidate before him, supposedly he was racist and the next Hitler. The Democratic political capital had already been spent on me with the last Republican president. I actually believed George W. Bush was Hitler at the time. If he wasn't, then he had to be some kind of demon.

So here we were in Los Angeles where Hillary Clinton could nuke the homeless and have children thrown to sharks for foreign money, but somehow it would be okay because it was better than Donald Trump, who was the *real* Hitler. Sure. The media started demanding the firing of James Comey. There was a 7% increase in the polls to Donald Trump; with every percentage point the media went more berserk! They wanted James Comey's head. How dare he investigate Hillary Clinton and tell the people about it! That was seriously the narrative around Los Angeles and on the television. Why was James Comey telling people that he was investigating Clinton? It must be an evil plot by the FBI to get a Republican president who will lower taxes. She was running for President of the United States. I would want to know if they are investigating her again. I quickly flipped my TV to CNN where they flat-out told me that it's none of anyone's business—just fucking vote for Hillary Clinton and shut the hell up! *Sure, okay, CNN.* Everyone seemed to think it was normal for CNN and every media outlet in America to tell people what to do. Nothing to see here—just the election of Hillary Clinton.

November 8, 2016

I woke up in my bed about seven in the morning and immediately raised my fists in the air, as I knew today was the day. Everyone will finally go back to normal. Hillary Clinton will take Obama's throne of doing nothing while enriching herself, and everyone will go back to talking about nonpolitical stuff like football. Celebrities will have nothing to talk about; topics like toxic masculinity, white privilege, one million gender stuff will all just fade into the background. Surely Hillary wouldn't set up any legislation for made-up mumbo jumbo like white privilege or toxic masculinity, and everything will be fine. Anything was better than the economy collapsing under Donald Trump as president. I was on a film shoot from seven in the morning till one pm. Today was a very easy day for everyone in Hollywood. Lots of people stayed home or got out of work early.

Many people I knew were not interested in voting for either candidate, so they were using the day as a beach or pool day. None of them actually told anyone that; no one wanted backlash from the unhinged Hillary supporters. The diehard Hillary supporters in Hollywood were militant. If you dared to say anything about their queen, there would be an attempt to turn your whole life upside down. Luckily, I didn't give a shit; I was posting information on Hillary Clinton all day, every day. I was probably the most blocked person in Los Angeles. I was very open on social media and in public about my disdain for Hillary Clinton and her corruption. I wasn't going to be bullied into silence. There were attempts to stop me from working with certain companies and certain people. Sure, I lost some acquaintances, contacts, and money along the way, but I didn't care. If my free speech was a deal breaker for them, then it wasn't really anyone I wanted to work with anyways.

Fuck these people! I told myself at this point. I wasn't going to be silenced into a Hillary Clinton presidency. That's the kind of shit that happens in third-world countries—it was not going to happen to me. It was really getting strange out there. But it was *all* about to be over; they could have their first woman president. She would do nothing but sell out the country for speech money. This country had withstood thirty to forty years of that already, so what harm could another eight years bring? Hollywood would return to talking about normal stuff, like if anyone saw Kim Kardashian fall on Rodeo Drive instead of talking about how racist white people were. Before I went home, I pulled over to a liquor store to buy tequila. I also couldn't forget to pick up a loaded Styrofoam box of nachos from Pepe's restaurant. This was going to be a night I wanted to forget, so there was no need to stay up late to watch the whole thing. I was going to be wasted before the first state was awarded to Hillary Clinton.

But before I did that, I dropped everything off at my house and went back out to vote. I arrived at the little church in my voting district and no one was there. I was surprised. I expected to see a Hillary Clinton party going on. All I saw was one or two voters—*okay then*. I went into my little voting booth, and I did what was important and what was right, by raging against the machine and voting for Jill Stein.

I turned on the news; CNN was already predicting that Donald Trump had a 15% chance of winning. *Wow, that's really high for him.* I got a call from Juan, my Hispanic friend I knew since I first arrived in Los Angeles. I lived with Juan and his family for one year before I set out on my own. "Yo, you gonna vote? Come over after," Juan said.

"I voted already but there's really no point; it's gonna be a predictable night." As I was saying that, I heard CNN say it would be a landslide victory to Hillary Clinton for about the fourth time in thirty minutes.

"Well, come over anyway. I'm almost home from work," Juan said.

"Who you gonna vote for?" I asked.

"I'm just going to write in Bernie Sanders," Juan said.

"Yeah, I would have done the same but Jill Stein needs 5% of the vote to get some kind of funding next time around to be in the debates," I replied.

"You like that woman too much," Juan said.

"If lightning strikes and Hillary loses Florida then I'll come over," I said.

"She just lost Indiana. That's your hillbilly state," Juan said. I looked up from my plate of nachos and tequila, and there it was—CNN had Indiana. The red state where good ol' boys drive tractors and chase chickens was going to Trump.

"Well that's not a surprise. That's probably one of the few states Trump will win," I said.

"I don't know if she's gonna win, bro," Juan replied.

"Yeah and maybe the sky isn't blue and the grass isn't green," I scoffed.

Juan laughed. "Lots of people hate her," he said.

"No one is gonna vote for Donald Trump. Trust me," I said confidently.

"Okay, well let me know if you are coming over," Juan replied. I put down my phone and my attention immediately went back to Wolf Blitzer on CNN. Here they were. For the last year CNN had been salivating over the idea of Hillary Clinton becoming president, and now they were predicting a landslide victory for her. She had been given a billion dollars, endless positive coverage, and excuse after excuse for her corruption at any sight of bad judgment. Anyone who dared question not supporting her on social media, or in public, was to be shunned from society. I had done a pretty good job of being shunned in Los Angeles. CNN marched on predicting utter failure of Donald Trump and an epic win by Queen Hillary Clinton.

This was about to be real life. And then...Hillary Clinton lost Florida. My posture straightened up from my couch; I had a mouth full of nachos that I tried to swallow too quickly. I began to choke and cough. I quickly called Juan. "Hey, did you see this?!" I asked excitedly.

"I told you, bro!" Juan replied. I stood up from my couch and threw my fists in the air. Yet I wasn't sure if I should be happy. *This was scary!*

"I'm coming over!" I told Juan. I tried not to get my hopes up, down, or any which way. I drove fast on the freeway, as I thought, *This is no big deal.* It's probably just going to be closer than I thought it would. *Keep cool. Keep calm.* I arrived at Juan's house and swung open the door.

"Wooooo!" Juan cheered as he sat on the couch with his dentist assistant girlfriend who was still in her scrubs, and our Black friend Augusta who was known for always wearing flashy metallic windbreakers. His dad owned a popular BBQ restaurant chain in Los Angeles. When Augusta was around, it usually meant he was there to sell us weed or cocaine. He was a good guy but made a lot of bad decisions despite that his dad owned the best BBQ business in LA County.

"This dumb nigga bout to be president," Augusta said.

"She's going to lose, dude!" Juan said enthusiastically.

"Nahh. She won't lose, but it's fun to pretend," I replied.

Juan's roommate Manuel walked in from the kitchen. "Hey, Trump just won Florida. You should start hiding now," Juan told him.

"That Cheeto won't win," Manuel replied. Manuel was an illegal immigrant who lived in Chicago, and then he came to Los Angeles when he was given a six-figure promotion. He wasn't a dishwasher. He didn't pick vegetables on a farm. He was given a promotion to be in charge of marketing for an online business that moved set props all around the country. Manuel has no college education and wasn't particularly bright. There wasn't anything special about this guy at all, other than he's illegal. He made a little over one hundred grand a year. I knew lots of illegals like him who never really fit the mold of what liberals thought they did. One time he showed me the fake social security card he had bought for five hundred bucks. For some reason though, I never really thought about it much.

We drank, ate, and watched as CNN went on predicting Hillary Clinton's glorious victory. Over and over again CNN reported that Florida wasn't anything, just a bad mistake on their part. And then state after state began to go to Donald Trump with only a few states going to Hillary Clinton. Everyone's mouths were open, as if we were watching a ten-car pileup on the freeway. Juan couldn't believe it. Manuel couldn't believe it. Augusta couldn't believe it. And I definitely couldn't believe it. It looked like CNN's Wolf Blitzer was going to have a heart attack. I was teetering on the brink of happiness that people in America saw the truth and was half worried to death that all my money was going to be taken by evil corporations.

Then CNN announced Donald Trump was becoming president of the United States. Juan, his girlfriend, Manuel, Augusta, and I all sat in the living room shocked, not saying a word to each other. I drove home with the music off. I never drove anywhere without music or radio. I was unable to really make sense of what was going on. I pulled into my driveway, went inside, and got into bed. I laid there awake, until morning came. I went outside with the same clothes on, as the morning sun began to rise on Los Angeles. The world was different; I could feel it. I could almost see it. Something in the air that morning was different.

And Now the World Was Changed.

Everything seemed new. November 9, 2016, was a new day unlike any other. All the world knew. People took to social media to talk about the election of Donald Trump, but there was something else going on. The day was different. The air was different. People were different. I took a timeout from trying to meet writing deadlines for myself and anything and everything in between. I drove to downtown Los Angeles and went for a walk. People were doing business as usual. Chinatown was roaring along with buyers and sellers, hagglers and tourists. All the trendy bars, breweries, factories, and production studios were running just as they would any other day. And while it seemed that it was the conversation that was different, because it was, that wasn't it. Something was just inexplicably different. We knew just by looking around that something irreversible had happened.

Suddenly, the stock market went crazy high. *Why would people be buying stock?* I asked myself. For the next two weeks, I didn't do much. All I could do was lie around and think. It felt like the whole world was falling apart. Donald Trump was now president of the United States? Donald Trump? *Donald Trump?!* Surprisingly the stocks kept skyrocketing instead of crashing. I couldn't understand why. This guy didn't pay his employees just because he didn't feel like it. Why were people buying stock; were they freaking insane?! Perhaps we'd all be moved into concentration camps, moving boulders back and forth, until we paid off all of our debt.

Maybe Trump would get rid of the minimum wage, and we would all be working for two dollars a day like in Mexico. I'd have to get out of California, because it was already too expensive for millionaires living here, and I was not a millionaire. My whole life was about to come crashing down at my feet, and it was all Donald Trump's fault. Maybe there would be a war with North Korea. I became so consumed with curiosity and fear that I began to constantly imagine different dystopian futures. All I knew was that Donald Trump won, and Queen Hillary Clinton lost. Oh god, why did I *not* vote for Hillary Clinton?! Yeah, she was a monster, but she was a liberal monster. She would have at least gotten rid of college debt. She would have at least initiated universal healthcare or free college.

I turned on CNN, because they will now have to admit their mistakes. They will give hope to people. This will be their time to finally be honest about their biased coverage for Hillary the past few months and go back to being a trustworthy news organization. This will be a moment in history that we will all remember. And what did CNN say? CNN said that Donald Trump didn't actually win because Hillary Clinton won the popular vote. They also said that Donald Trump didn't win because there was Russian collusion. *Collusion?* I had never heard that word before. Then they said Donald Trump won because white men told their wives to vote for him. *What the fuck?!*

Then CNN said that America voted for Trump because white people are racist. This was not a legitimate news network any longer. One crazy extreme out-of-touch person after another went on all these news channels to say the most asinine things I had ever heard. CNN was cancer. Then all of the news channels began saying it, and they became cancer too. This Russian collusion stuff made no sense. The whole thing sounded hokey. In fact, the whole thing came from

Hillary Clinton talking about it at a debate. But maybe, just maybe, CNN was right for a change; maybe there was something to it. *Anything to save us from Donald Trump*, I thought. The story was that Donald Trump Jr. met with a Russian lawyer from the Kremlin to talk about dirt she had on Hillary Clinton.

If Hillary Clinton didn't want dirt spilled about her, she shouldn't do dirt. Why were all these TV channels telling me that no one should be allowed to find dirt on Hillary Clinton? The coverage was 24 hours a day. It was nonstop Russia, Russia, Russia. This Russian lawyer they had, who was supposedly connected to the Kremlin, was just a Russian lawyer and had no connection whatsoever to the Kremlin. It would be like the Russian media saying that I had ties to the White House. I'm American and that would be my only tie. This was a giant stretch for CNN but by this time I was getting used to fact checking every little thing that CNN said.

The meeting they had amounted to nothing. Also the charge of collusion wasn't a charge at all. It wasn't a crime to meet with other countries to talk, even though that was not really what happened. Hillary Clinton met with Ukraine to talk dirt about Donald Trump, and they said *nothing* about that. In fact Clinton even paid a British spy to collect dirt on Trump—but there were no charges of collusion there. So what was this bullshit they were running with 24 hours a day? Just like the whole campaign circus, I couldn't make sense of how illogical this was. Democrats were buying all of it though. To make things worse, Los Angeles had become unhinged. People were losing it out here.

Protests were everywhere; they consumed downtown Los Angeles. Feminists, Black Lives Matter, Environmentalists, LGBTQ, liberals of all types were all out protesting in unison. I drove into Chinatown to pick up pastries with my girlfriend, and when I looked across the street, I saw someone familiar walking to a protest downtown. I ran over to see if it was real. I came up close to her and I could barely believe it. "Hey, Jacquelyn? Jacquelyn?!" She turned around and was wearing a black T-shirt, jeans, and very short hair. "Jacquelyn?" I asked.

Her eyes met mine with an anger I never saw from anyone before. I always knew her as such a sweet woman. Her clothes were a departure from her sunny pink dress that I saw her in at the art gallery dinner. I noticed a sign she was holding that said, "White silence is Black genocide." *That's a bit extreme.* She didn't speak but her face and eyes were so angry. It was bizarre. Suddenly the sign was pushed out of the way as it made room for little bitch boy Dory who stood there wearing the same outfit as Jacquelyn. Dory commanded, "Back away from Jacquelyn, I'm her white ally, and I will protect her with violence from your white supremacist ideologies if I have to!" *What the fuck was this guy talking about?*

"That's the dumbest shit I've ever heard," I said. Dory turned away from me, towards the coffee shop we were standing next to. Dory spoke up, getting the crowd's attention, who was dressed similarly to him. He said, "This man is a white supremacist, who once defended America at a restaurant in West Hollywood! He just tried to attack my friend Jacquelyn because she is an African American lesbian!" *She's not a lesbian*, I thought.

Jacquelyn tapped Dory on the shoulder and whispered, "I'm not a lesbian." Dory shushed her and whispered back, "It's okay." Dory looked over the crowd as if he was some kind of holy preacher. "Let this white supremacist know that we won't tolerate his hate towards our African American lesbian sisters!" The whole crowd turned on me with the type of sickness I've only seen in zombie movies. "Fuck white supremacy!" They screamed over and over again. The chant got very loud very quickly, as some of them surrounded me saying the same thing in unison. I looked at Jacquelyn, and I could tell she was not present. She looked around and saw these people chanting and began to chant with them. Her mouth was going through the movements, but something other than her brain was controlling her.

I was so confused and scared by the whole thing that I quickly backed away. I ran across the street as two of these very scrawny, pale men ran beside me and continued the chant. I got to the sidewalk on the other side of the street, and one of them grabbed me by the shoulders. Out of instinct I squared directly up with him and kicked him right into the dick, like it was the World Cup of soccer. He fell to the ground holding his crotch, as the other one backed away. The others continued their stupid little chant. I went inside where my girlfriend was ordering doughnuts. "Everything okay, Daddy?" she asked. I was a bit out of breath but fine.

"Just catching up with some old friends," I said. I began double locking my doors at night. The days drew closer to Donald Trump's inauguration and so did the hysteria. I was very upset. Everyone I knew and trusted for so many years on the television had lost their minds. Michael Moore was blaming white privilege, and Bill Maher was blaming Russia. Robert DeNiro just kept yelling, "Fuck Donald Trump!" Everyone had lost their minds out here, and it was just a matter of time until we would soon all be looking for food in trashcans. It was only the socialist Bernie Sanders who could help us.

After a lot of stress and worry, I called my dad. He's a truck driver. We talked a bit as I was trying to make sense of things, but eventually I just asked him, "You think everything is going to be okay?"

He let out a giant laugh, "Yes!" He voted for Trump. I couldn't believe it. But I could tell, he thought I was being just as hysterical as everyone around me. *Was I though? No way!* How could more capitalism be a good thing? Capitalism is what caused the recession. I remember it clear as day; I was sitting in San Francisco and reading stories from CNN about how capitalism doesn't work anymore. CNN is *still* a news organization and not everything they say can be that biased, right?

One of my favorite movies of 2015, *The Big Short*, said that capitalism was to blame too. How could Brad Pitt be wrong about the recession? Obviously, we needed socialism to save us from this. Donald Trump was going to throw gasoline on the fire and finally crash our economy down to ashes with *more* capitalism. That totally makes sense. I'm always right about politics. Socialism is the only way we get out of this mess. A few days later the radio said that the stock market was higher. *Higher? How?!* Won't these idiots lose their money when the stock market crashes? The whole world has gone mad! There must be a way for Bernie Sanders and socialism to save us.

Meryl Streep and Her Golden Globes Speech

I grew up in the middle of nowhere, Indiana, and I had to learn about the rest of the world through watching movies. I was fascinated by actors, writers, and directors, because they were the wise ones. They knew everything. All of their movies with interpretive meanings that led people to believe that America is greedy and bad made me smarter—they were so interesting and cool. All of it *had* to mean something, and all of it *had* to be true. Although I had to admit, after being around these people for six years, the allure was kind of wearing off. You don't really understand how far removed from reality these people are until you live and work around them.

I worked on a music video with Snoop Dogg once, and he wouldn't show up until the production team bought him Popeye's chicken and Skittles. People in America have this perception that celebrities in Hollywood are the "chosen" people and so did I until I got here. No. They are the children of millionaires and billionaires, already famous artists, business executives, investors, inventors, or people who work in the industry in one capacity or another. A best friend or family member can get you a long way. Of course most of the actors don't want you to know that their aunt is Julia Roberts or that their mother runs craft services for a TV series. It takes away from the glamour and the idea that they achieved their position from their own brilliance and impeccable perseverance and achievement.

Things have worked this way since Hollywood and the music industry began. Slowly it became what it is today, which is about 99% nepotism, 1% crazy fluke stories of random good-looking people getting a job because they were at the right place at the right time. Robert Evans' movie career started by getting noticed when he got out of a pool. Of course the 1% are the kind of stories you want to hear about and the ones Hollywood makes sure you do. They are the most interesting, inspire hope, and spread the general belief that anyone can be anything, which is the backbone of American society. This was all a lie that I began to resent. The longer you live in Hollywood, the more stories you hear. Jonah Hill growing up friends with Dustin Hoffman's kids isn't as interesting as homeless Jim Carrey writing a check for one million dollars and keeping it in his back pocket all his life. For Jonah Hill it worked out because he's talented. But a lot of fat, funny people who don't know Dustin Hoffman's kids could take his place in a second.

There have been many more with the same opportunity who were only adequate and somehow were still capable of pulling off a ten-year career. Not a lot of fame is really based off of talent, although it can help. It's all an illusion. It's entertainment, so it's supposed to be a closed door for everyone outside of the bubble; when you know the right people, your adequate talent can be magnified to seem excellent even when it isn't. Meryl Streep's mother was a famous fine artist who worked at Home Furnishings, and her father was a pharmaceutical executive. It's the same linage that all of them have, and there are many more who have great grandparents and great-great grandparents with the same lineage. Hollywood is full of kids who didn't want to do anything, so their mommy and daddy got them an audition for (fill in the blank).

Most actors either deny it, hate talking about it, or are just completely ignorant of it. Many movies, tv shows, and musical bands are filled from top to bottom like this. Maybe you aren't even passably good looking or as talented as Meryl Streep. Maybe you are obese and have an acne problem. If your dad owns the Chicago Bulls, they will at least let you hold a boom mic. Actually they will probably let you produce. You can make six figures to a million a year just standing around. This is the way it's always been and the way it will always be. Since the recession and the advent of technology made independent films less financially viable, it works like this but even more. It's extreme now because there are less opportunities.

People like Obama's daughters have to find a job somewhere, so a spot at Miramax Films is always on hold for them. When you see a speech like the one Meryl Streep gave at the Golden Globes in 2017, you see how much they've bought into their own delusions. You see how people like Meryl Streep think that the world couldn't muster going on without her. In Meryl Streep's mind, she's the reason the earth spins. Many of us in California, in the arts, and on the left fall victim to this line of thinking. The more gold statues we get, the more confirmation we get that we are the moon, the stars, and the reason the sun rises.

I had seen this severe narcissistic personality disorder for about six years in Hollywood and about five in San Francisco. I wasn't one of those types of people though, *oh no*. I only looked in the mirror to look at my fat ass a modest six times a day, instead of a dozen. No one told me anything or I would flip a table on top of you. Get out of the way, assistant at CAA, the noble Bernie Sanders socialist who's going to save the world is here! It was early and we had already arrived at a Golden Globes party in West Hollywood. We had all been having a few drinks and everyone was on the roof of this apartment building in tuxedos and dresses. No one in *real* independent film actually had tickets to the Golden Globes, but we dressed like we did anyways.

I was brought downstairs by a producer friend, Stacy, who I had been working on a project with the last few months. Stacy has a lot of freckles, and has a personality you wish all girls had. She pulled me inside a laundry room and my buzzed brain immediately began thinking sex. "Eww, gross," she said. I stepped back.

"What?" I asked.

"Why are you talking to...that...person up there?" Stacy asked. I smiled.

"Oh jealous much, are we?" I asked back. I came forward again to Stacy but she held me off with her hand.

"Ugh, you are drunk," she said. Now I'm definitely confused and a little angry.

"What is it?!" I asked.

"That....girl you are talking to," she replied. I smiled.

"Oh, Esmerelda? Don't worry about her, she's cool. But if you don't tell me why you brought me down here to an empty laundry room, I might have to take her up on her offer of going back to her place tonight." I said. Stacy grinned, giggled, and nodded.

"Oh, I bet you'd like that!" she said. I smiled and continued to push forward on Stacy as she held me back with her hand.

"Sure, she's kinda sexy but not as sexy as you," I said. Stacy grinned and giggled again.

"I'm so flattered that I'm sexier to you than a *man*!" she said with her eyes were wide open for more shock value. I stopped, stood up straight, and suddenly I was sober.

"No." I said.

Stacy nodded. "Yes!"

I shook my head, "No!"

"Yes!" Stacy yelled back.

"But she looks..." I almost said.

"Like a man?" Stacy asked.

"*NO!*" I yelled. Stacy very quickly grabbed me by the shirt and got so serious all her teeth were showing.

"Listen to me, Roland! Whatever you do, act normal! She...or whatever...has many friends in the skyscrapers of Burbank! If *she* or....*it*....finds out you don't want to sleep with her because she's—you know— (coughs) we will both be blacklisted!"

"WHAT?!" I frantically asked.

"Yes!" Stacy screamed. I slapped her hand from holding my button-down shirt.

"I don't play those stupid blacklist games!" I yelled. She grabbed me by the shirt again but this time very hard.

"Roland, I do! Listen to me for once!" she said.

"But—*it*' *s* a man!" I yelled.

"Don't say that! It's a woman!" she replied. Stacy tried to calm me down by patting me on the head.

I whispered. "But...it's a man," I said.

"Shh! It doesn't matter! Donald Trump is president," she said. I sighed. She had a point. Now that Donald Trump was president, everyone had to toe the line in Los Angeles that seemingly only the LGBTQ community knew where it ended.

"Fuck," I said. "Shh!" She said with her finger to her lips. We walked up to the top of the roof with Stacy pushing me up. I grabbed my coat off of a table and turned around to see a tall Latina man in a silver sequined dress. Her curly hair was obviously wigged. This was Esmeralda standing right in front of me. *How many tequila and Diet Cokes did I have?!*

"Hey!" its voice loudly said in a very convincing way. "Why did your friend take you downstairs? Was it because you were talking to me?" Oh shit, it knows!

"Um, no. She just reminded me that we have a big day tomorrow," I said. *It* looked me up and down.

"You don't seem as drunk as you were before; maybe you need a drink at my house?" she/he said as it touched me on my neck, with its long silver gloves, more aggressively than ever.

"Uh, sorry I can't," I said.

"I'll walk you downstairs then," it said.

"Oh, you don't have to," I answered.

Esmeralda grabbed me by the arm, with a very stern, serious man's voice, "I'm walking you downstairs!" Half of the party looked over. *Oh shit. Am I in trouble?* I walked downstairs as fast as I could with her right behind me. It was so quiet and awkward as people went past us upstairs. I didn't want people to see me. It was four flights of stairs and I had gotten to the bottom floor first since she had heels on. I went outside and waited. *If I'm polite, I can wait to see what she has to say, and all will be forgotten.*

Esmeralda threw the door open and walked up to me like a cowboy. "Tell your friend I'm all woman, more than she will ever know, and that the next time she outs someone who's transgender without their permission, I'll pull her fucking hair out," he ordered. His voice then suddenly went back to sounding like a woman. "Okay, bitch?" she said to me.

I was stunned and also very confused. "You're mad at her for telling me you're a..."

Esmeralda turned ghetto on me quickly, waving its finger in my face. "Oh, hell no! You are not going to misgender me today, sweetie! I'm all woman!" I had no idea what was going on.

"Don't blame her for telling me something I would have found out on my own," I said.

Esmeralda scoffed at the notion. "Bitch, my pussy looks like Ariana Grande. So you best keep both of your mouths shut, okay? If word gets out in this town that you two are transphobic, it's over for you!" it said as it walked away towards the door of the apartment building. I couldn't believe it. Donald Trump ran for president and won, and now Los Angeles was being run by some hierarchical order of transgendered men who we were forced to pretend were women.

I slowly backed away and then lightly jogged to my car when I was out of sight. By the time I got home, I turned on the TV and there she was—Meryl Streep accepting the Cecil B. Demille award. I began to take off my suit as I listened to her speech. Trump was to blame for Hollywood not having enough Black actors now. Of course there was more misinformation about anything and everything from a person who knows nothing. Black movies were a niche market. This was business. The age range that went to see movies in America was white men 14 to 30 years. It was a huge percentage of the American population; that's who spent money and whose money you had to get.

That's just the reality of the American population who goes to watch movies. But of course this was now Trump's fault. Everything was. I got in bed to forget all about it. Then suddenly I got a call from Stacy. I answered and she said excitingly, "Oh my God, did you hear Meryl Streep's speech? It was amazing! Do you think we should hire more African Americans for Tyler's movie?!" she asked. She was so gleeful and dense at the same time. The producer of a small indie film had called to ask me if we should hire more Black actors for a film set in France in a castle in 1500 A.D. I went to sleep thinking the hype would be over, but of course it wasn't. Everyone loved Meryl Streep and this totally out-of-touch speech.

And all of Hollywood, as far as I could tell from their social media and casting calls, were now hiring based on skin color. Over the next few weeks I even saw "Whites need not apply" on ads for executive positions. Society had done a one eighty in discrimination now. The funny part was that Esmeralda got one of these highfalutin six-figure jobs about two weeks later. She checked off two categories, Hispanic and transgender, and of course the most important check box, she was sleeping with one of the executives. Supposedly she led the guy to believe she would tell his wife and kids if she didn't get the job. Esmeralda went back upstairs to the party that night, and she took home another filmmaker. He later got one of his screenplays optioned. Stacy said she should have never told me Esmeralda was a man. I've had screenplays optioned before, and sleeping with a woman who has to shave her back hair isn't worth it. That filmmaker still doesn't have his movie made.

The Women's March

"Another protest?! No way! This is enough protesting!" I said. It had been two months of protesting, and now my feminist-lesbian-community-college-professor neighbors wanted me to drive them down to the protest of all protests: The Women's March. I had driven them to two protests in the past month. All four of them were beside my front porch as I sat on the steps with my groceries smoking a cigarette. "Take Uber!" I told them. Goldie was the owner of the house next to me, the only car owner of their household, but she had a DUI recently. She had very light milky skin, short fried blonde hair, and her dimples pierced. She rented rooms to the other three girls.

"That's like forty dollars, dude," Goldie said. I rolled my eyes.

"Yeah, dude, and that's exactly how much gas I'll be spending if I take you," I replied.

"Pfft. You drive a hybrid. When did you become so cheap?" Goldie asked. Tanya, Goldie's longest tenant and friend who constantly dressed like she's Wednesday from the Addams family, responded in monotone.

"Is it because your Asian girlfriend won't let you?" Tanya asked.

"It's because I'm sick of the protests!" I explained loudly. The other two girls were normal looking enough because they are still new tenants and hadn't been influenced by the other two yet. They were quiet and stared blankly at this whole fiasco.

"Are you like a Trump supporter now?" Goldie asked. Being called a Trump supporter in Los Angeles is like people thinking you have the type of STD that doesn't go away. I had to shut that down immediately.

"Nooo! I'm not a Trump supporter!" I said.

"We aren't asking you to go, dude, only to drop us off," Goldie explained.

"We already told everyone on our podcast we will be there to livestream," Tanya said in a concerned way. I'd rather get a lap dance from a drag queen, like the time I took them to Gay Pride, than to take these women to another protest. The music they made me play when I took them somewhere was atrocious. But they were my friends and neighbors, and I knew they really wanted to go. I also knew they probably wouldn't shut the hell up until I finally agreed.

"Fine. I'll take you. But no aux cord," I stated. They all looked appalled.

"No aux cord?!" Goldie asked hysterically.

"You *are* becoming an old white guy," Tanya stated.

"No shit!" Goldie replied.

You could almost hear their daddy issues when they spoke. The Women's March started early Saturday morning. I woke up and took my Hybrid out of the driveway that morning at exactly 7 a.m. and drove to the side of their house. Of course I had to wait about twenty-five minutes for them. It was only fair since I'm a white male oppressor who was taking them to the Women's March for free. Finally, here they came, the most sophisticated bunch you'd ever see—they were all wearing pink pussy hats and holding repulsive signs. We had to show the whole world what winners we were here in Los Angeles. They all got in, Tanya sat in the front and the other three piled up in back. "Yeah...do you have to have those hats on during the drive?" I asked.

"These are cool," Tanya said.

"Cool isn't the term I'd use for them," I replied. We drove down the freeway with all of them talking obnoxiously loud about how much they hated Trump. He's racist, he's sexist, he's Hitler reincarnated, he's all the typical stuff you'd ever hear from a bunch like this. I could see Los Angeles coming up on the freeway. *As soon as I get there, I can kick these girls out on their asses.*

"Oh! You know what I wanna hear? I want to hear 'Who Run This World?'" Goldie said. All four girls clamor together with one big "Yeah!" I quickly went into survivor mode.

"Nope! We all agreed on no aux cord for me to take you here," I replied.

"Actually *you* said that, but *we* didn't agree," Tanya said.

"Nope! We have an FM station playing at a moderate level, and that will have to do till we get there," I said.

"Dude, what is wrong with you?!" Goldie asked.

"It's like these white guys have gone back to the fifties already with this asshole being elected," Tanya said. I tried to put on a fake smile as I pretended to not go insane.

"Seriously! You've changed the past few months," Goldie said. I sped up as the city was getting closer. "Oh my god, dude! I'll give you twenty dollars for gas," Goldie said.

"It's thirty dollars for gas and you should be giving me that anyway, miss independent woman," I replied.

"But...we are girls!" Goldie said. All four of them clamored together again, "Yeah!" I couldn't believe it. After all the years of hearing these women talk about equal rights for women, which I repeatedly told them they already had, they were now saying they shouldn't have to pay for their ride to the Women's March because they are *girls*. I pulled out my aux cord and gave it to Tanya.

"It's 20 dollars for this aux cord, take it or leave it!" I said.

"Taken!" Goldie screamed. I smirked. I was proud of myself. Los Angeles was right in my sight, and I had gotten one over on them. But *of course*—for the next forty-five minutes, my car only moved two miles! I was on the 10 freeway, with Los Angeles only four miles away but was stuck in traffic listening to Beyoncé's "Who Runs This World?" ("Girls!") I sat there with this awful music coming out of my car speakers, as four feminist pink pussy hat-wearing university professors sang along to the song. *Shoot me now!*

So when I found my opportunity to get off the freeway, I took it. I took the streets the rest of the way to downtown. I dropped them off a few blocks away from where the march started. As they all got out of the car, I asked Goldie for the twenty dollars. Goldie slammed the door and then took her flappy boobs from her sweater and laid them on my window. *Typical.* But as a white male I probably deserved it for oppressing her with my presence in my car on the ride over. I watched her and her roommates walk away laughing, as my attention quickly turned to the people who were shoulder to shoulder walking in the streets.

There were so many naked people, so many insane costumes and signs. There were so many marchers with those disgusting pink pussy hats. All of them were here for one reason and one reason only: they all hated Trump. How dare a rich billionaire have sex with women. Talk about a monster, right? I finally got away from downtown and got back on the freeway. It was I who knew the real reason they should be mad. I was far more educated, articulate, and had a master's degree in fine art. These people should care more about fighting for free healthcare, free education, free housing, and universal basic income.

If we could just get independence from the corporations and only work if we chose to work, instead of work because we have to, then we would have *real* freedom and control of this country. Then we wouldn't be slaves to the system, because the system would be a slave to us. We should choose and decide the fate of our lives, not corporations. Because after all, we are the richest country in the world, the richest country in all of history. I nodded in agreement with myself. It's a curse being this smart.

What did shake me though was why I was in the minority of people who believed we could have all this stuff. *Why didn't Bernie Sanders win?! And more importantly, how did Orange Man win?!* It made me mad just thinking about it. Yes, demon Hillary Clinton wasn't perfect by a long shot, but maybe we could have at least gotten universal healthcare with her. But *Trump?!* Weren't these people sick of the corporations taking all the wealth, leaving none of it for the rest of us? I didn't get it. These Trump supporters must be brainwashed. They must drool and appreciate working sixteen-hour days in some hot factory for ten dollars an hour. We were being ruled by morons, and yet the ones who were supposedly "resisting" were more concerned with if Trump said the right thing or not. We needed to save America with socialism before it was too late, not yell at the sky like an animal!

The Inauguration

I made sure to pop by the liquor store for tequila and Cheetos, and then of course I stopped for a big takeout of nachos from Pepe's. This was going to be an inauguration I wanted to forget. I drank and ate, depressed by the fact that it seemed poverty, war, and oppression of people wouldn't end in my lifetime. I watched as Donald Trump was sworn in and as he gave his speech. In his speech he said, "We will no longer surrender this country to the false song of globalism." *Hmm, that's interesting.* I took a swig of tequila and Diet Coke from my rocks glass. That's odd. What does he mean by "false song of globalism?"

I knew NAFTA and TPP were horrible trade deals. I knew when NAFTA was signed that it was supposed to send jobs over to Mexico, with the idea being that helping the country and its people would potentially help America. However, I also knew that failed miserably. Jobs that were supposed to bring people out of poverty only paid its workers two dollars a day. So not only did it not help them much, it didn't help us. I repeated the Trump line out loud, "We will no longer surrender this country to the false song of globalism." *That's a good line.* I didn't exactly know what it meant, but I liked it. So I said it again, "This country will no longer surrender to the false song of globalism." *Interesting.* But I scoffed. Everyone knows we shouldn't be giving our jobs to other countries.

Bernie was going to stop the same thing. I watched on as it became nighttime in Washington D.C. There was a march of soldiers who went past Trump as he watched. They saluted the now newly inaugurated President Donald Trump. I squinted at Trump as I couldn't believe my eyes. I saw it in an instant, and then the camera cut away. I picked up my remote and rewinded my DVR. There it was again; Trump was holding back tears. "What the fuck?" I said out loud. I never imagined Donald Trump having feelings. I thought he just threw money around all day, snorted coke, and fucked playboy models. Not only was he crying, but his crying seemed genuine. I rewinded it again. It was hard to know what to make of it. This old man must really have a thing for the military. I scoffed again. God! This guy is going to raise the military spending. Unbelievable! That's the last thing we need—more money going to the already oversized and overpriced military.

These Republicans loved their military, but they hate, hate, hate using the money on the people who voted them in. It bugged the hell out of me. However, there was this one thing that kept popping up in my head since Trump won. Every once in a while, I heard a voice in my head say, "Maybe you're wrong." I scoffed at that dumb voice. "No!" I said out loud as I talked to myself. There is no way we have money for all this other stuff but not have money for the people to have food, shelter, and healthcare. *No way!*

Then another thought popped into my head that I couldn't get rid of since Trump won. *Was it even possible for the country to pay for all the stuff I thought it could?* I never really looked it up for myself, but it didn't make sense that it wouldn't be possible. Rich people were just greedy. There's no way Bernie Sanders, Hillary Clinton, Barack Obama, virtually all of Hollywood, and the most trusted names in news on CNN would advocate for things we couldn't pay for. They were all at least smart enough *not* to do that. That I knew for a *fact*. I was absolutely sure of it. *So tie those thoughts up, put them in a basket, and send them out to sea.* Those thoughts aren't needed. However, it would be nice to see the facts for myself. But I can surely sleep well at night because all those people did the research for me. Those evil bastard Republicans wanted people to starve to death because they were poor and worked shitty, meaningless jobs. I hated them so much!

Project Veritas

As soon as Donald Trump won the election, CNN and the rest of the news channels began the Russia narrative. They went as far as insinuating that Donald Trump was a Russian spy. And over the months it kept building, and now that Donald Trump was actually president, that's *all* they talked about. Any hint of Russian vodka or Russian salad dressing within a five-mile radius of Donald Trump meant that it was obvious treason and that the president needed to be impeached. We were two months into the Trump presidency, and that's all we heard. Everyone around me in Los Angeles loved talking about it too. Trump had even dropped a few bombs on Syria, Russia's ally, and CNN went as far as to say that he only did it to confuse people to make them believe he wasn't a Russian spy, when in fact he was.

They had also begun a special investigation led by some tall, lanky guy named Robert Mueller. Hillary Clinton came out and gave her first interview, giving 39 excuses as to why she lost the election. Three to four of the excuses had to do with Donald Trump being a Russian spy, who did the horrible, unbelievable thing of telling people that Hillary Clinton cheated Bernie Sanders out of the primary. How dare anyone commit the horrible crime of telling the truth about Hillary Clinton. I began referring to Hillary Clinton as the hidden Queen of America. She really seemed to be, but the only problem was that no one voted for her to have any power at all. However, at times she seemed to have more power than Donald Trump, who *was* President of the United States.

With all the corruption surrounding Hillary Clinton, there was still no *real* investigation on her. This was frustrating since Donald Trump said she'd be in jail if he were president. I was totally fine with that. It was almost like he had very little power at all. The whole thing was just so shady and corrupt. For two months in Los Angeles, everyone around me would tell me that Donald Trump was a Russian spy, that he colluded with Russia, and that there was a tape of Russian prostitutes peeing on him. They said that Vladimir Putin had this pee tape and would show the world if Trump ever said no to him. These people were driving me nuts, and they would get mad if I dared to question their logic. How could they believe this nonsense? They were so sure of *all* of it, and they couldn't believe that I dared to disagree.

I was at the Hollywood Roosevelt, with a group of three that included Stacy from the Golden Globes party. We were sitting at a booth near the bar on Friday night, after watching dailies from the French castle film I had done rewrites on. All three of them were getting hysterical as they just couldn't fathom that I didn't believe that Donald Trump was a Russian spy. I was so used to the hysteria by these people at this point that being calm and rational was easy for me, and in turn could usually calm some of their outrage.

The director of the film, a tall blonde swoopy-haired skinny tie-wearing fellow named Tyler, barked at me, "Oh my god! Oh my god!" he said.

"Look, I understand everyone is still upset about the election, but Russia did not elect him, America did." I calmly explained.

"He met with Russian oligarchs!" Tyler yelled.

"Stop saying Russian oligarchs," I said back. Stacy was to my right sipping on her martini.

"I never thought I'd see the day where Mr. Anti-Capitalism *American Slave* author would be defending Donald Trump," Stacy stated. Greg, a fat, balding, bearded producer who usually did commercials, was sitting across from me next to Tyler.

"How can you make excuses for a man who participates in wage slavery?" Greg said. *Ugh. I hated the way he just said that.* He sounded so disgustingly woke. I hope I didn't sound like that.

"Because Donald Trump is not a Russian spy!" I said loudly as the whole bar looked at me. Tyler squinted at me suspiciously.

"Maybe you should write a book called *Russian Slave*, because that's what you sound like right now," Tyler said.

"Oh, good one! Or maybe I should have my dad give me two hundred and fifty thousand dollars to make a film in a French castle," I replied.

"Hey, my father says he's going to take away my car if I can't pay him back by next year," Tyler replied, sounding very worried.

"The Audi R8 or the Bentley GT?" I playfully asked. Tyler stared at me very seriously and concerned.

"...I'm not sure yet. Probably the Audi R8, if I can convince him the GT was driven by Macklemore that time in Vegas." I smirked at the rest of the table, but none of them seemed to be aware I was joking. They were all very displeased Hollywood Hills people. They weren't from Indiana like I was, and they never had bologna sandwiches and macaroni and cheese for dinner.

I woke up the next morning, and there my vindication was blasted all over social media, which was Project Veritas. I had heard of this guy before. He had done some undercover stuff before that was pretty crazy during the Obama years, however I was indifferent to it then. But now he's got CNN producers on hidden camera admitting that the Russian scandal is a hoax, and it was all over social media. He even had CNN commentator Van Jones say on hidden camera that the Russian scandal was a "nothing burger."

"Yes! Yes! Yes!" I said out loud. I was so excited. I rushed to social media to post. I tagged Tyler, Greg, and Stacy on Facebook. I was supposed to meet them in just a few hours for a night shoot for Tyler's film at a sound stage. I couldn't wait to see their faces when they saw Van Jones say the Russian scandal was a "nothing burger." I was so happy with myself, because it was verifiable proof that the media's Russian scandal was bogus. CNN's own producers and anchors said it was a hoax, and not only did they say that but they said they were doing it all for ratings. I was on my way to the sound stage in Anaheim where we were shooting, and it was about six hours after I had posted to Facebook.

I checked Facebook in anticipation as I drove to see if they had responded. I saw nothing. *That's strange.* I thought for sure that I'd see some angry but funny responses from them. I thought for sure that they would have to admit that I was right. However they hadn't said anything. *That's weird.* This put an end to the Russian scandal that they were so concerned about. This should be a good thing. I checked CNN on my phone as I drove, and they seemed to be acting like Project Veritas didn't exist. It was odd. CNN's own producers and anchors were caught on tape saying that they were lying to the American people for ratings, and nothing was being said about it.

The CNN producer specifically said that ratings were the reason for the 24/7 Russian scandal. But to CNN this didn't exist. It was like we were in the early 90s, and to CNN the internet didn't matter yet. They were ignoring it. How could they ignore what was all over the internet?! I got to the Anaheim sound stage we were shooting at, and outside the fence where we usually got in stood a three-hundred-pound bald security guard who I knew quite well. He asked to see my ID. I kind of frowned at him. "ID? You don't need my ID," I said. He pretended to look at his clipboard. He then looked out over me as if he didn't want to see me, for what he was about to say next. "Uh, yeah...you're not allowed on set today," he said. My mouth dropped.

"What?! What do you mean I'm not allowed on set today?!" I asked.

"I'm just following orders," he said. My jaw seemed like it was unattached to my face.

"Whoooaaa, this is crazy! Get someone out here right now!" I yelled. The security guard's movements became frantic.

"Let me see," he said.

"NOOO! There's no we'll see! Get Stacy, Tyler, and Greg out here right now!" I demanded. The security guard threw up his hands.

"Ok, ok, ok, let me talk to Stacy or Greg," he said. The security guard pulled out his walkie talkie and then walked away from me so I couldn't hear him. I saw the crew pulling out a jib from one of the trucks inside, so I instantly knew it would take at least two hours to set up. I knew they were not busy as this was almost a full crew. The security guard came back about two minutes later and sighed before he spoke. "They are *all* really busy right now," he said.

"Busy doing what, eating at the craft service table or nursing their hangovers?! I'm serious! You better fucking get one of them out here before I lose my mind!" I said.

The security guard nodded, "Just calm down, okay? Just calm down. Give me one second." The security guard walked away and called them on the walkie again. I could hear his concerned voice. The security guard came back sighing. "Stacy is coming," he said. I paced back and forth fuming. *This is so fucking ridiculous.* About five minutes later Stacy slowly walked out and came towards me on the street.

"No Tyler or Greg?!" I asked. Stacy held her hands together as if she was a teacher trying to *not* have a confrontation with her student. "Everyone's really moody right now," I smiled condescendingly. "Oh come on, you three saw the post I tagged you in on Facebook, it destroyed your whole worldview, and now you're mad!" Stacy scrunched up her face and squinted.

"The video was edited," she said. I belted out a huge laugh.

"Is that what you're telling yourselves?!" I asked. Stacy's face looked perturbed as she bit her lip. I loved it. "Stacy, if you are going to stand there and tell me that was edited then you need to find a new line of work!" I said. Stacy's face got even more bitter.

"Maybe you do," she said. I laughed again.

"So you're going to deny it, even when it's right in front of your face?!" I said.

Stacy tilted her head. "We aren't denying anything, we just have different opinions than you." I was about to explode.

"This isn't an opinion! The CNN PRODUCER SAID IT ON FUCKING VIDEO TAPE! IT'S FAKE! VAN JONES SAID IT WAS A 'NOTHING BURGER!'" I shouted. Stacy tried to use her calming rational voice on me like I did to them last night.

"But Project Veritas is a white supremacist website," she said. I felt like I was losing my mind.

"OH MY GOD! YOU PEOPLE ARE INSANE!" I yelled so loudly that I startled the three-hundred-pound security guard. Stacy put her hands out as if she was guarding herself from me.

"Okay. Please leave or I'll have to call Anaheim police," she said. I started laughing again.

"I rewrote this piece of garbage so you could actually budget and shoot it!" I said.

Stacy said very calmly and collectively, "And we appreciate that, but as you know you aren't needed on set." *These scumbags.* Even though she was right that they didn't need me on set, I wanted to take my hybrid and ram it into her BMW. This was the new world we now lived in since Donald Trump became president. Everything was racist and white supremacy they didn't like.

Even if you have proof that the bullshit they believe in is false, it doesn't matter. It was like these people had joined a cult. I left the Anaheim soundstage and called my friend Brian. I went to an empty bar on Hollywood Blvd and started drinking, until the only other rational person in California I knew got there. Brian was from Indiana like I was, and he moved down to Southern California around the same time I did when his parents moved here. I had never seen delusion like this before, and it seemed like Brian hadn't either, but since he had always been conservative maybe he was used to this or something. I was beginning to question everything. The sound of protest drums and chants coming through the doorway got my attention as Brian walked in. "Are they protesting again?!" I asked.

"Didn't you know Donald Trump was a Russian spy?" Brian asked back.

"Oh god!" I said.

"My parents say they are moving back to Indiana," Brian said.

"Really?!" I asked.

"They can't stand it here," Brian said.

"And this has only been a few months," I said back.

"And it's only going to get worse," Brian replied.

"Surely these people will wake up," I said as I took a drink. Brian sat down at the stool next to me and began smoking his American Spirit cigarette. This was one of the only bars in LA where you could smoke.

"This is the socialism you wanted, isn't it?" Brian asked.

I scoffed. "No! None of those people even know what socialism is!" I said, perturbed at the notion.

"And you do?" Brian asked in a rare moment of being a dickhead. I turned to him mad, outraged like one of them even.

"Yeah, I do. It's the workers sharing in ownership of the profits and not just someone at the top making all of the money," I said.

"I bet if you asked the people outside you would get fifty different answers," Brian replied.

"Uhhh yeah, because they don't understand what socialism is," I said, pissed off.

"So they all think they know what socialism is, and you think you know what it is; how do you actually think that's going to work?" Brian asked in all sincerity. I turned back around on my stool, faced the bar, and drank my drink, in a rare moment of not having anything to say back. I pretended to look at my one thousand-dollar iPhone, as I pondered his question. I never logically thought out the revolution before, however I knew I didn't want to be on the same side of those morons outside.

Charlottesville

The summer went by with beach parties, cookouts, and club hopping from Hollywood to Palm Springs. Politics was on the tip of everyone's tongue, because every few days it was another news story about Donald Trump that had everyone talking. In Los Angeles you could find yourself doing anything, and at this moment we were at a small gymnasium watching midget wrestling. The crowd oohed and ahhed. Juan looked up from his phone and said to me, "Hey, some girl got killed at a Nazi rally today." I looked at him.

"That's horrible," I said. And then the rest of the night we drank until we all came back to Juan's place. Everyone was there, including my friend Brian, Juan's illegal immigrant roommate Manuel, and our friend who was the Black son of the BBQ King of Los Angeles, Augusta. My movie-making colleagues Tyler, Stacy, and Greg even came by and pretended not to be mad at me for proving them wrong about Russia. My Cambodian girlfriend Hong and my lesbian professor neighbor Goldie were also there. No one really said anything else about what happened in Charlottesville for the rest of the night.

Juan was cooking shark out back at 2 a.m., while the rest of us were laughing in the kitchen. And that's exactly my point. None of us had said a word about Charlottesville. It was one white guy who stupidly sped his car into a crowd and killed one white woman while trying to get away from counter protestors. Obviously, this is sad and tragic, but the truth was that it should have been a non-event. Any other year it would have been a blurb on the news. It would have been a story you passed by to read about your favorite NFL team's preseason. Any other presidency and it would have been exactly that. For so many years, out of every news station, all people heard was that *all* Republicans were racist. That one I knew was a lie. Brian was a Republican and he wasn't bigoted at all. I shit you not, Brian cried one time because of a PBS documentary on racism. But no one else I ever met that was Republican was racist either. Why would anyone hate someone because of skin color in the year 2017?

That wasn't a part of people's lives in modern-day America anymore. Here we were in a house of all different races and backgrounds, having fun, and not thinking about what the world wanted us to believe. But the past year or so under Trump's presidency, the mainstream media, who lived in the small bubbles of Manhattan and Beverly Hills, reported that racism was everywhere. To them racism was within everything and there was no escaping it. Cows were racist because their milk wasn't chocolate. If your waitress was Black, choosing white bread over wheat bread was racist. Do you think any of those things are *not* racist? Well guess what, now you're a racist too! Don't ask questions as to why, just believe what they say to believe bigot! And to them, Trump was the racist of all racists. It didn't matter if it didn't make sense; truth didn't matter. The only thing that mattered was what these supposedly very smart journalists on TV said, even though they came from rich, out-of-touch families. But for those four to six hours that night, when we were busy having fun, busy not caring about the worldviews of TV anchors who had ten million-dollar apartments in Manhattan, you could see how simple all of it really was.

By the next morning, that all went away of course. The media had a job to do, and their job was to pump up the volume. We woke up at my house where Goldie fell asleep on my couch watching TV (probably CNN or MSNBC), despite the fact her house is only a few yards away. Goldie walked into my room that morning with nothing but a sweatshirt on. "Dude, did you hear about what happened to the girl in Virginia?!" she said. I could barely open my eyes as I woke up next to Hong. I looked at my doorway and saw Goldie half naked standing there.

"What?!" I asked.

"This is serious!" she said loudly. I scoffed at her.

"A girl got hit by a car two thousand miles away. Go back to sleep," I told her.

"Yeah but these are Nazis!" Goldie loudly explained.

"Nazis?! No, they are gym teachers with nothing to do on the weekend," I told her. Goldie huffed and puffed and then stormed out, which I assumed would be the end of it. I woke up a few hours later and saw that it was 1 p.m., which meant I had slept half the day away. I walked into my living room and couldn't believe what my eyes were seeing. Every corner of my living room was filled with hand-crafted, sparkle-filled protest signs, with Goldie and monotone Tanya working on them. I looked around in awe. "You've got to be kidding me," I said. They looked at me as if I just told them that Lady Gaga's music sucks. Goldie pointed at me as she kneeled on the floor.

"If you aren't outraged right now, then you are the problem!" she said. It was by far the most unoriginal thing these people said up until this point.

"Why are you talking like a politician?" I asked.

Goldie yelled loudly, "There are Nazis out there killing people!" My hand met my face; I couldn't take this. I grabbed the remote off my couch and turned on the TV. The channel was already on CNN, and the first thing that came up was a video of out-of-shape men who were supposedly Nazis marching with tiki torches. CNN inserted scary horror movie music into the background, as the tiki torch marchers yelled at the night sky. I saw their bellies hanging over their belt buckles, and I couldn't help but to laugh out loud. "You are such an asshole!" Goldie yelled.

"Because I don't freak out at plumbers armed with tiki torches when the TV tells me to?!" I yelled back.

"Why are you always talking like a Trump supporter now?" Goldie asked in all seriousness. I threw my hands up.

"Everyone who disagrees with you is a Trump supporter?!" I screamed.

"Stop taking his side!" Goldie screamed back.

"I'm not taking anyone's side!" I said louder.

"There are Nazis in the streets!" She retorted, trying to outdo me. *I'm so sick of this shit.*

"Goldie. There are no Nazis in the streets. There are three hundred and thirty million people in America. Do you know how many of them are members of hate groups?" I asked. Goldie stared blankly at me. "Less than ten thousand. It's less than one percent," I said to her.

"They are out on the streets though," Goldie explained empathetically.

"And the only reason you think that is because the TV wants you to," I explained.

"There's no talking to you!" Goldie screamed as she threw down one of her markers. I scoffed at her.

"Why are you even doing this here anyways?" I asked as I stood up to get a closer look. I saw paint all over my antique Persian rug. There was speckled blue and pink paint everywhere. "Goldie! Please tell me I'm dreaming right now!" I screamed.

Goldie screamed back, "You're dreaming right now!" I sighed.

"Just take all of this shit back to your place! Please!" I said. They eventually got all their stuff together and finally left. Once they did, I started looking into this supposed Nazi rally that they were so obsessed with. Right away I began to see how hard it was to get any *real* information on this event at all. I had never seen such an attempt to control a narrative in all of my life. Stuff would slip out little by little, by their own missteps, or by people who were actually there, and then it would quickly get wiped from the internet. Weren't journalists supposed to be unbiased and searching for the truth? The media didn't want you to know *why* he drove his car into the crowd or *what* he was doing driving down that alley.

They didn't want you to know that police said he broke down and cried when he was told that he killed someone. Nazis aren't supposed to kill anyone unintentionally—they are supposed to do it with a smile on their face while pledging allegiance to the Third Reich. However that's not what he did, and the media didn't want you to know that. The information was out there, but to the common person who just read headlines and didn't compare or contrast mainstream news articles with independent journalists, or for people who took everything at face value, none of that mattered. James Fields Jr. was an evil racist Nazi pig, and that's exactly how the supposed truth-seeking mainstream journalists wanted it. The reality was that despite the marching with tiki torches, and scary tone of music under the CNN edited montage, this twenty-year-old security guard wasn't a Nazi at all.

No one there called themselves a Nazi or any of the other things that the news media said. Yes, the media had this long list of people who said he's a horrible person, and maybe he was considering he killed someone either intentionally or unintentionally. But let's add some context that the media isn't interested in you knowing. This twenty-year-old kid who was leaving a protest to keep a confederate statue, was trying to get his Dodge Challenger out of a small alley surrounded by ANTIFA, who viewed him as being responsible for all the evil in the world. When an ANTIFA leader David Dixon armed with a military-style rifle screamed at protestors to attack through the alley, just thirty minutes prior on videotape, they did. A few fists or key scratches to his car is no excuse for what he did, which is why he sped off into the crowd in front of him; but to say he did it on purpose because he's a Nazi isn't intellectually honest.

He agreed to life in prison to avoid the death penalty and, the way the media portrayed this, there wasn't a chance in hell he would have ever received a fair trial. Even if there was verifiable proof that he was some saint (which he wasn't) before he did what he did, it wouldn't have mattered. He was a Republican Trump supporter, and the media wanted him *dead*. A trial would have meant the death penalty no matter what. And why wouldn't ANTIFA attack? Wouldn't you attack if you just *knew* this twenty-year-old kid was the devil in flesh and bone? If I truly believed someone was that evil, I would have attacked too. The people ANTIFA attacked were not Nazis. They were a bunch of people protesting the taking down of a confederate statue, being met with anti-racism-obsessed counter protestors who thought everyone who dared to want to keep a confederate statue up must be a Klansman and a cross burner. CNN said that was the case, and why would CNN lie? They were the most trusted name in news.

The next two days, there was a romanticizing of these AK-47 wielding ANTIFA members that seemed to stand alone amongst all the hysteria. CNN were their biggest cheerleaders. ANTIFA are mostly young, college students all over America, who want to destroy the government, tear down statues, and burn the American flag. They were praised by CNN for fighting the supposed Nazis for *weeks*. Later Donald Trump gave a press conference where he rightfully blamed both the skinny-jeaned college hipster group ANTIFA and the supposed Nazis who were gym teachers for what happened in Charlottesville. These were two groups of people who were set up to think that the other was Satan coming out a crevice of earth.

This was Trump's statement as he reminded the media that he condemned hatred and bigotry for the eighteenth thousandth time:

As I said on – remember, Saturday – we condemn in the strongest possible terms this egregious display of hatred, bigotry, and violence. It has no place in America. And then it went on from there. (The only part the media cared about –>) Excuse me, they didn' t put themselves down as neo-Nazis, and you had some very bad people in that group. But you also had people that were very fine people on both sides. You had people in that group ‑ excuse me, excuse me, I saw the same pictures you did. You had people in that group that were there to protest the taking down of, to them, a very, very important statue and the renaming of a park from Robert E. Lee to another name.

Of course CNN and all of the rest of the mainstream media didn't seem to care about his condemning of hatred and bigotry for the *second* time of this event, and the millionth time in total, since his campaign started. To them, Trump was Hitler reincarnated, and they saw it as their job not to deliver the news but to make everyone see the same things they did. For the next two weeks, it was like living amongst programmed robots. From the TV to the internet, to the guy at the pot shop, everyone was talking about racism in Trump's America. People were sharing memes comparing what happened in Charlottesville to World War II's D-Day, and they were doing it in complete seriousness. How could anyone compare one white guy running over one white woman with a Dodge Challenger, to D-Day World War II? I sat there and stared at the meme in the middle of the night in my dark living room on my laptop. It was at that moment, I realized that the vast majority of America had a much lower intelligence than I could have ever imagined.

I watched YouTube videos of these ANTIFA kids in Berkeley, a city I once lived in, and saw them break windows and set cars on fire. Then the most jarring of it all was when I heard them speak of socialism. Some of them espoused ideas of socialism being no borders, no country, and paying for the whole world's stuff. Some of them argued that socialism was about killing white people, since they had all the money. Some of them even praised Stalin, Mao, and Pol Pot. Pol Pot had a special place of hatred in my heart, because my Cambodian girlfriend and her friends had recently told me horror stories of his dictatorship in Cambodia. My girlfriend's brother starved to death. One older Cambodian lady, who was my girlfriend's friend, told me how when she was little her parents would have her steal food from Pol Pot's army so they could survive. My girlfriend showed me the history of Cambodia and it's era of socialism through movies and documentaries. That wasn't real socialism, because it would work here in America. It had to work, because America was the richest country in history.

I hated these pussy ANTIFA kids who called themselves socialist. These kids tore down American statues, were against freedom of speech, and praised despicable dictators, Pol Pot, Stalin, and Mao. How could anyone like those people? I only liked Fidel Castro and wore his T-shirt because of Oliver Stone's awesome documentary about him. I thought Oliver Stone was one of the good ones in Hollywood. Oliver Stone couldn't be wrong, could he? Why are these ANTIFA kids calling themselves socialist? It reminded me of what Brian said to me at that empty bar in Hollywood. That's not what socialism was to me; what they were describing didn't sound good to me at all—it sounded like evil. Surely there were socialists who wanted what I wanted and who knew what real socialism was, like Bernie Sanders and I.

Million-Dollar Football Players Kneeling

The Charlottesville event was the longest, loudest, and most delusional of all the Trump-deranged hysteria up to this point. No one seemed to grasp what was fully going on. It was molehills being made into mountains, but it eventually died down right around the beginning of the football season. So here we were after what was perceived as the most racist moment in history also starting an athletic sport with 70% Black athletes. There didn't seem to be much of an outcry for diversity in the NFL for some reason. Over the past year or so, a few football players would kneel during the national anthem because of supposed social injustice. These football players drove Maseratis and beat their wives; somehow they always seemed to just get a slap on the wrist. We were supposed to believe something was unjust for them and America was to blame. Of course all the news stations *loved* it.

Colin Kaepernick, who once drove an unconscious woman to a hospital and dropped her off in the grass, even wore socks with cops depicted as pigs on them. Donald Trump seemed to feel how most sane people felt. Trump was giving a speech and, as usual, didn't give a flying fuck what anyone thought. Trump loudly asked at one of his rallies, "Wouldn't it be great if they fired one of these sons of bitches when they knelt for the anthem?" The whole crowd cheered. And why wouldn't they? Trump had said what was on everyone's mind. Conservatives like Trump knew the FBI statistics, because the right-wing news had always told them. I had known FBI statistics table 43-

A, because I had investigated it for myself after getting my car broken into a half dozen times in certain neighborhoods. You begin to notice certain patterns after a while.

Obviously, each community of people has its own set of problems, and we should always be looking to help each other whenever we can. However if you have a criminal record, a gun, and resist arrest from police, that's not a *me* problem, that's a *you* problem. And to say that communities with skyrocketing crime is all the police's fault, or America's fault, is about as false as false can get. We all knew the truth. Most of us have been brow beaten to never dare tell the truth out loud. The word racist is like a magic spell for white people; when someone accuses a white person of racism, we shrivel up into a ball and beg for mercy, even when the claim is ludicrous. However for the past year, everything was considered racist.

There were articles saying that if you had white children, then you were racist. There were articles claiming that white people who had dogs were racist. One article said that white people who said "Good morning" were racist. There was also an article claiming that the solar eclipse was racist, because only people in white countries could see it. I think that one was satire, but they were all so absurd that you couldn't really tell. It was the first time I began googling white people, just to see the current news articles about us. Suddenly my European ancestry was very popular. It was one preposterous story after another, but from social media to common interactions, white people said nothing. I mean what if someone called us racist for being offended that the news was calling us racist? White people were scared to say anything about being called racist, because if we did then that might be racist. The whole thing was hilarious, sad, and sickening at the same time. I for one was tired of *all* of it.

I had started seeing these articles after Trump won, and I began seeing them more and more since. But after Charlottesville, it was like the training wheels were off. I began seeing the most racist conspiracy theory garbage I had ever read. It was like I was reading something from the nineteenth century, only it was in 2017, and it was about white people. I couldn't believe newspapers like *The New York Times* were getting away with publishing this trash. I also began noticing a certain pattern with the names of journalists writing this. These white women from broken homes must have *really* hated their fathers. You also couldn't forget the scrawny hipster dude journalists; I knew a few who I went to college with who were writers for these rags. They were all like Dory, who were all so full of white guilt. They kept writing this garbage to a largely silent white population, surrounded by people from other countries. They let them in through immigration, because we had been told the past few years that diversity was our strength. I began to notice a few immigrants I knew in Los Angeles on social media, and they ate this stuff up. America was the one letting them escape from the horrid conditions of their original country, and now the immigrants hated us for it. It was sad really.

So of course people cheered when Trump talked about firing kneeling football players who were egged on by ethno-masochist journalists to hate America. America was *not* the reason for their problems. America was the reason they were paid fifteen million dollars a year to throw a football. I sat there when the news ran the video of Trump saying it, and I even wanted to cheer. I was a liberal–socialist citizen who had contempt for America my whole life, but even I was sick of this shit. I was blamed for every problem under the sun the last year, just because I was white and because the majority of white people voted for lower taxes. I wasn't responsible for the way they voted. I voted for Jill Stein but now it was a racial issue to Democrats. *Get the fuck out if America was so bad.* Wait, did I just think that? I would have been sent on an airplane years ago if that's how we handled these people.

However I was beginning to appreciate America a lot more with so many people shitting on it. Imagine if I immigrated to China, and after a few years said, "You know what? China sucks! And straight Chinese men have privilege! Give me money on top of the money I'm already receiving because I'm white and oppressed!" I don't think I'd fair too well. Actually, I'm not sure if there's any country I'd fair too well saying that in, except of course America. They could come here and say whatever they wanted about me, my family, my ancestors, *and* America, yet I was supposed to stay quiet and thank them on my knees. I love freedom of speech, but these same people were saying that any disagreement with them was hate speech. *What the fuck?!* All people were supposed to stay quiet and be shit on daily;

after being shit on, we were all supposed to say "Thank you" to the third world immigrant or inner-city criminal, because diversity is our strength.

And here we were at the beginning of the football season, about to see something so unbelievably delusional. I watched the Dallas Cowboys, who were America's football team and whose players made millions of dollars, along with ultra-rich owner Jerry Jones all kneel for the National Anthem in unison. I watched the Pittsburgh Steelers' entire team stay in the locker room for the National Anthem, as one player came out by himself and stood bravely because he was ex-military. CNN was pissed! So that football player actually apologized afterward. He *actually* apologized for standing for the National Anthem.

Doesn't everyone love a good Facebook argument? I finally snapped. I couldn't take it. That was when any ability I had to stay quiet finally collapsed, as if I ever had that ability in the first place. Juan and our Black friend Augusta were on Facebook arguing about who was more oppressed by white privilege. *Is it Hispanic people or Black people who are more oppressed by white privilege?* I went to the comments section of their argument, where Juan seemed to insinuate that white people stole America from Mexico; so in his opinion, Hispanics were *more* oppressed by white people. I couldn't take it anymore. "White people didn't get here by magic; they were pioneers," I commented. I had just lost 30 followers in an instant on Facebook. I did the unthinkable, horrible thing of being white and pushing back on the narrative that I was responsible for all the evil in the world.

Our friend Augusta, who had a profile pic of Barack Obama, went on with the usual clichés about slavery. "America was built by slaves!" he commented.

"Only one percent of the population owned slaves. The average slave would have cost 40 grand by today's standards. America was *not* built by slaves. No one owned slaves except for people like the Bill Gates of that era," I replied. Juan retaliated in an effort to help his misinformed cocaine-dealing friend.

"America is the most racist country on earth!" Juan typed. I laughed as Juan *had* to know that wasn't true.

"Juan, last time we visited Mexico we saw comic books with giant-lipped Black people eating watermelon. And shit, Mexico didn't even deem Black people citizens until 2016!" I replied.

"You're white so you wouldn't understand!" Juan commented.

"Oh I see. Because I'm white I don't understand you, but since you're brown, you absolutely understand me?" I asked.

Augusta came back with what should crumble any notion that he was oppressed by white people. "You're just mad because you come from a poor white family!" he commented. I never thought of my family as poor; I thought of them as good people. Period. But it was funny that the cocaine-dealing Black son of the Los Angeles County

BBQ king thought that. Maybe I forgot to reciprocate with buying him a drink at a club one night. Maybe it was because my parents actually worked, unlike his. But wasn't *he* supposed to be poor and oppressed by me? It didn't make sense. I couldn't help but laugh.

"Wait a second, but I thought I had white privilege?" I asked.

He typed back quickly, "You never got pulled out of your car by the police and thrown on the windshield!" Augusta replied. I nodded in agreement as I read it. That genuinely made sense to me.

"You're right, I never sold drugs in my life, and I've never been arrested for that," I typed back.

"Fuck you!" Juan replied.

"Dumb racist piece of white shit!" Augusta typed.

Wow, that escalated quickly. And racist? Augusta actually does sell cocaine. I wasn't trying to be inconsiderate of Black people. He just happened to be Black and sell cocaine. How is it racist to state what is factually correct? I was never arrested for selling drugs, because I don't sell drugs, but he was arrested, because he does. And even if I was arrested for something, I definitely wouldn't dare call the arresting LAPD officer a honkey, which is what Juan told me he did. He's Black and I'm white; he sells drugs and I don't; and those are the facts. *Is it racist to tell the truth?* Juan and Augusta seemed to think that every problem in their life was a result of their skin color instead of their decisions. "Who was teaching them this?" I asked out loud in front of my computer. I silently knew the answer.

After that, Juan and Augusta blocked me from Facebook. I was terribly sad that I would no longer be able to see their highly intellectual debate of who was more oppressed by white people. It was at this point that I realized that the media was correct: racism was alive and well in America. However, it wasn't the type of racism they were talking about. Then of course came the cherry on top. Manuel, Juan's illegal citizen roommate, must have been watching us from *his* Facebook page. I hate how Facebook shows every conversation you have to the entire world. Manuel posted directly to my Facebook profile page, "White people stole this land!" Manuel's profile page then disappeared, as he had obviously blocked me as well. An illegal immigrant—who illegally had a job, after illegally buying someone's stolen social security card for five hundred bucks, and then illegally made six figures a year—thought he had more of a right to America than I did, as an American citizen. This was the United States of America in October 2017.

Obama's Portrait Artist

About two weeks later, I had finally calmed down and didn't want to pummel any skinny jean news journalists or boomer hippie TV anchor that pushed this bullshit twenty-four hours a day. I was at home when I opened my laptop, and I decided to allow myself to read the news again. I saw *The Washington Times* article that revealed Obama's presidential painting had been finished. *Oh cool, I bet he will have a good one,* I thought. *I can read this; it won' t be a problem.* I told myself. It was a portrait of Obama in a chair, with a wall of leaves behind him. It was a bit awkward looking, but nothing like his portrait artist's previous work. The Black portrait artist that Obama picked had done a few eye-opening paintings before the presidential portrait.

The most interesting one of all—you might need to sit down for—was a painting of a Black woman holding a white woman's decapitated head. Yes, I said that correctly. Obama had picked a portrait artist who had multiple paintings of a Black woman holding a white woman's *decapitated head.* A few news websites went on to explain how brave and forward thinking this portrait artist's previous artwork was. This was all portrayed to be normal; it was all just normal that the first Black president had picked a portrait artist who had multiple paintings of a Black woman cutting off a white woman's head. I shutdown my laptop, as I wondered how exactly I could have voted for that guy. For some of you big Obama lovers, who think he and his wife are just so amazing like I once did, this may be hard for you to digest unless you see it for yourself. Google Obama's portrait artist and click on images. Enjoy!

Thanksgiving

It was a few weeks before Thanksgiving of 2017. I woke up to check my Facebook, and I saw one of those stupid memory showcases that Facebook does. It was from three years ago. It was a picture I posted of an American Indian from the 1800s. I was disgusted with myself, as I had no doubt posted it to be edgy and cool. I had no doubt posted it to say to the world during the time of Thanksgiving, "Oh this is the Indian's land, look how un-American and cool I am for acknowledging it." *Gross and stupid. I was such an idiot.* Why did I even think something so stupid? My girlfriend Hong got up a few hours later, and she dragged me to different stores as she shopped.

Hong has very unusual shopping tastes. After all of the Chinese grocery stores and jewelry stores, we somehow ended up at a Hobby Lobby of all places. I was complaining about wanting to leave, and I somehow found myself in Hobby Lobby's huge pro-American section, where it was aisle to aisle with America-themed decoration for living rooms. That's when I saw this huge framed replica of the Declaration of Independence. I looked at all the names that signed it so long ago and realized that I had never really thought much about the beginning of America.

That's when a *real* memory crossed my mind—well, sort of. It was the memory of watching the TV series *John Adams*, with Paul Giamatti playing the main character. I had watched the show quite a while ago when I was still living in San Francisco, but I remembered how well it captured all they went through to create America. It seemed like America beating England in war back then was like a high school football team beating an NFL super bowl team. It wasn't at all possible to win, but somehow, they did. Something in me emerged I had never felt before. Suddenly it was like this framed replica in Hobby Lobby was pulling me towards it to buy it.

On the way home I told my girlfriend Hong all about John Adams and how America began. She listened along with a glimmer in her eye, and strangely she told me some stuff about it that I didn't even know. *Huh, weird.* When I got home that evening, I placed the framed replica of the Declaration of Independence over my couch; it looked good. I never would have expected that I'd be doing something like this in my thirties. It felt odd, but it felt kind of good too. I didn't quite understand why conservatives always loved America so much and why liberals didn't, but since Trump won, it was like liberals wanted to burn the US to the ground. America just needed to change to the way America really should be, which is a more socialist country; and it should turn to my way of socialism of course, not the ANTIFA idiots' idea of socialism. *That's not real socialism.* It was all very confusing.

I hated that ANTIFA called themselves socialists. Surely John Adams would have agreed with me, right? Maybe I should watch that TV show again. I stared at the Declaration of Independence over my couch. *With Thanksgiving coming up, I better not see any anti-American Thanksgiving posts on Facebook this year.* I better not see some idiot like me post a freaking American Indian either. Everyone better enjoy their bullshit pumpkin pie and shut up. I had been disinvited to numerous Thanksgiving parties and dinners all around Los Angeles. I didn't care, I was tougher than that. If these people loved their TV news anchors who told them to hate America, white people, and whatever else, well then, I was *all* for it. Let CNN have them.

I wasn't going to be bullied into submission by skinny-jean-wearing ethno-masochist whites. I decided this Thanksgiving I was going to do what I had always intended on doing; I was going to look at the economics of America and find out if all this socialist shit I had always been told about and believed was even possible. Since the day I was born, I had been fed so many lines about the amount of wealth in this country. All the celebrities I looked up to like Michael Moore and Bill Maher told me it was possible and morally good to help everyone we can, and that socialism was the way to do it. They had always been smart people...they just... hadn't been very smart the last few months. Trump had broken them or something. Bill Maher was obsessed with Russia, and Michael Moore's fat ass was screaming about white privilege.

Even so, surely they wouldn't advocate for expensive unaffordable stuff if it weren't possible. They most likely would do their research before advocating for it all over television for so many years. There's no way they would call for all these universal programs unless they were 100% certain. *Right?!* Suddenly I had many more doubts that I had never had before. The Democrat protesters and politicians were so crazy and dumb the past few months, and the more and more I talked to these people who called themselves Democrats, liberals, progressives, or socialists (it's all the same now really), the more I began to wonder if they were the dumbest people on the planet.

Some of them seemed to think America could feed the whole world. Some of them seemed to think that the whole world should be allowed to come to America and have free health insurance. There was no limit on their altruism. I kind of didn't want to be associated with these people any longer. And I definitely wanted them to stop saying they were socialist! So I had to do what it seemed like no one on the left ever did; I had to see if any of this shit was even possible. Socialism had to be the answer some way. Luckily, I knew just the person to help me. He's someone you'd never guess someone like me would ever be friends with.

Possum Mike McDowell

He now worked as some kind of accountant for the US Military and government. I'd explain it to you, but I'm too smart to understand what the hell it is, because I'm a liberal. We are all too smart to explain things like this. The more I thought about how smart I was just because I was a liberal–socialist–Democrat voter, the more it sounded like absolute bullshit. None of these racism-obsessed people seemed smart at all, but somehow, they all thought they were. His name was Mike McDowell, but his nickname was Possum, however I couldn't remember why. He didn't start out as the type of person who would join the military at all; in fact, he was the *last* person you'd expect to join the military, even over me.

He arrived at San Francisco the same day I did, for our first semester of college in the summer of 2005. He was quite possibly the weirdest dude I ever saw in the Bay Area, and this was only my first day of five years in San Francisco. He had giant gauges in his ears and bleached blonde hair that was turned into a giant Mohawk. The sides of his hair were shaved and dyed jet black, and he had a big bull ring in his nose. His jean jacket had the arms ripped off, with black marker and patches of bands all over it. He was a photography major and I was a film major. I didn't look as punk rock or as rebellious as Possum Mike McDowell, but I probably tried and failed miserably a few times in high school. At the most I wore a lot of black, a Che Guevara or Fidel Castro T-Shirt, with earrings. I dyed my hair sometimes and wore bracelets but that was about all I could pull off.

He was from Iowa and I was from Indiana, and yet we both looked as if we had been in California our whole lives. I guess that's television for you.

We both stood in line at the school's office as we received our student IDs. I guess this is the moment in a Hollywood movie where something happens, and we meet each other and become great friends. Nothing like that happened. He tilted his head out of line, let out a big belch, and that was it. Over the next two years, I'd see him in the hallway, cafeteria, or at parties where he'd either be very quiet or hanging off the ledge of a roof with one hand, with his other hand holding a bottle of beer. It scared the shit out of me when he did it; luckily, he never fell. One time I saw him do it, and he couldn't get back up, so another guy and I helped pull him up. He was a very scrawny guy, just like most of the guys in California who lived off top ramen.

One morning after a party in Berkeley, right outside of San Francisco, I saw him walking to the Bart Station ahead of me, so I ran up to him; to my shock, it looked like he was crying. I had never really talked to him except for a few times, however I knew enough of him to know he was the last person I expected to be crying the morning after a party, or any time at all for that matter. I ran up to him and asked if he was okay. He said in his raspy voice, "Fuck off!" I let him walk ahead of me after that, and I got on a different section of the train than him. As far as I knew we rode into San Francisco together that morning.

The next two months I didn't see him at all, not in the hallways, or school cafeteria, or at any parties. I didn't think anything of it much, until I heard his name at the New Year's Eve party. It was a seedy apartment in the financial district of San Francisco. Beside the couch in the living room were two guys from school in front of a glass table snorting cocaine. That's when I walked in, sat down on the black leather sofa, and heard one of the two guys on the right in mid-conversation say, "Lasted longer than McDowell at least."

The other guy on the left laughed, "Anyone could last longer than him." He snorted. This immediately sidetracked any plan of hitting on the blonde girl next to me on the couch.

"Hey, do you know what happened to him?" I asked as the two laughed.

"You knew him?" the one on the right asked.

"Uh, not really. Sort of. Why?" I asked. The two laughed some more.

"He was a complete loser! He went around looking all crazy, acting all crazy, turning in 35mm black and white pictures of dead cats, then get this—one night after a party, he quits school and joins the army!" The two then laughed obnoxiously loud. I was so shocked that I became instantly still.

"Wait......what?!" I asked as I shook my head in disbelief. Surely they misspoke as they giggled some more at my surprised face. The one on the left tried to contain his laughing but can barely do it.

"Yeah, a few months ago, he just up and joins the army like a total loser!" He then offered me his cut-up coke straw and I passed it to the girl next to me.

"Are you sure?" I asked, shocked. The one on the right killed a bug on the table.

"Yeah, we're sure, the whole graphic design department couldn't be happier. He came in screaming like a banshee at people every day—where have you been?" asked the one on the right.

The one on the left tapped him and said, "He's a film major."

The one on the right smirked, "Jesus, how many film majors are there?" They rambled on being condescending and crude to everyone and everything, as most art majors are. That's when I tuned them and everything else out, because I was completely and utterly stunned. I couldn't believe it; I didn't drink or do any other drugs that night or, for that matter, a few nights. I walked home, up the large San Francisco hill, to my Nob Hill neighborhood, in the middle of the night—alone.

I wondered for years what it was that provoked a 180-degree change in the guy known as Possum Mike McDowell and what happened to him. I didn't find out until I graduated and moved to

Los Angeles when I saw his Facebook profile. He was chiseled and muscular, with buzzed hair, no gauges, no bulls ring in nose, no mohawk or dyed hair, and not only that but...he was smiling. This guy was a human punk rock show from The Fillmore, and now he was chiseled, in army fatigues, and...*smiling?* Why was he so happy?! I never imagined the guy could smile at all, and after days of wondering I messaged him. We kept in touch for the next few years, but never did I ever talk to him about what exactly happened that night in Berkeley, California.

It was around the 2016 Republican Convention, when Donald Trump was nominated, that I saw the ex punk rock goth kid post a pro-Donald Trump meme. I was so outraged that my teeth began to grind. *How did this guy become so brainwashed?* However, he was in the Army now, so I didn't want to say anything. As the outrage of liberals dragged on and on, my frustration finally spilled over to social media, and we talked some about it; he even fought off some lefties from school we both knew on my Facebook page, who we both disagreed with that Charlottesville was like D-Day World War II.

It's silly I know, but it was kind of cool that this guy came from the Midwest like I did, and he was now eviscerating the same racism-obsessed liberals we used to get plastered with, who were now revealing themselves to be morons. He switched sides and now seemed smarter than all of us. It was June 2005 when I first saw him, and now it was November 2017. It had been twelve years since he changed on a dime after a party one night in the spring of 2007, and I just knew he had to know something I didn't.

We decided to meet up in San Diego, where he was based out of, since he was off from work for two weeks. Judging from his messages on Facebook, he was excited to meet and talk to me; it was like we were long-lost best friends. He seemed to understand something I didn't and was excited to share it with me. So I drove into San Diego with my girlfriend Hong, ready for anything. We met him right in front of his military base where soldiers were running up and hugging their wives and children, and he was standing there as buff as a professional wrestler, clean cut, from head to toe, with sunglasses, and a huge smile on his face. He grabbed and hugged both of us, and said, "Yes! The awakening has begun!"

I looked at my girlfriend kind of confused, as she looked at me smiling with no idea what was going on. He then hugged me one on one and grabbed me by the shoulders. "I'm so glad you are finally waking up from this!" he loudly explained. I was very confused so I just kind of looked at him and nodded. After a few hours of gambling at a San Diego casino, I was finally able to rip my girlfriend away from the baccarat table before she lost too much money. The three of us then went partying at a club in a high-rise building. My girlfriend went off to dance with all the girls on the dance floor. While she did that, Michael and I sat on one of those swanky V.I.P couches, where we got bottle service from half-naked waitresses.

Everything was normal and fun, and then he sat down and took a big swig out of the bottle we got, which is the type of thing I'd expect from Possum Mike McDowell. He screamed over the techno music so that I could hear him. "So, you ready for the truth?!" he asked.

I smiled, "After the last year I had, I wouldn't be surprised by anything!" Michael patted me on the back hard almost spilling the tequila and Diet Coke in my hand.

"It's all lies!" He told me with a grin on his face. I was startled a bit.

"You mean, like what?" I asked.

"Everything you've been told growing up, all the music you listened to, all the TV and movies you watched," Michael said. I smiled in a confused way again.

"What do you mean?" I asked.

"It's all hippie bullshit! What's happening now is Marxism from the 1960s in its final death throw from Trump exposing it," Michael said.

"Marxism?" I asked. He inched over to me.

"Thanksgiving is this week; you'll see tons of Indian pictures on Facebook proclaiming we owe this land to Indians," he said.

"I used to post shit like that all the time during Thanksgiving!" I told him loudly as I was surprised that we had the same experience.

"I know—same with me. It's all bullshit! They fill kids' heads with that—no country on earth is made to feel ashamed for conquering another land like Europeans in America," Michael said.

"And that's why you joined the military?" I asked.

Michael laughed, "Nooo! I had no idea what was wrong with me then—I joined the military because I wanted to wake up the next morning and look forward to something other than having my next drink." *That's quite depressing,* I thought, as I set my tequila and Diet Coke down on the table in front of us.

"You really shocked people in San Francisco!" I told him.

Michael laughed, "In San Francisco, the so-called artists slash baristas in the mission I use to hang out with, and they all thought I lost my mind! What I realize now was that I was finding it again!" I nodded with him as I tried to understand.

"I have to admit, the night I heard you left for the military, I stopped everything for a few weeks," I told him.

"Look, I know how it is, because I used to be you. You drink, fuck everything that moves, nothing means anything, and that's how they want it!" he said.

"I wouldn't say that's quite it," I replied. Michael nodded.

"You weren't as extreme as I was, I'll give you that. The stuff you did in school always had meaning. You aren't postmodern, which is a good thing," Michael said.

I didn't know what to say. It got quiet and awkward for a while, so I picked up my drink to sip on it. A few minutes later we took the elevator down to the bottom floor for cigarettes. There was nothing but San Diego lights, tourists, and the night life all around us. "You should join the military," Michael told me. I scoffed, "Me?! No way! I wouldn't last two seconds in the military—I'd be running to Canada after the first hour of basic training."

Michael laughed, "It's not that bad."

I mockingly laughed back at him, "Says Vin Diesel over here. You probably weighed 90 pounds when I met you in San Francisco."

Michael smiled and leaned back as if he was reminiscing on his San Francisco days: "I would wake up, smoke cigarettes, eat a bagel, drink whiskey, go to whoever's apartment was having a party that day, talk about how great Lenin was, drink whiskey some more, fall asleep, and do it all over again. All I had to do was make sure to pick up my financial aid check. I think my GPA was a 4.0." I nodded and wasn't surprised as he was always someone I knew was smart, despite the window dressing he always wore.

"Ha! I think it was higher than mine, and I actually tried!" I said as Michael laughed.

"I think you were the only one," Michael said as I shrugged.

"Probably," I said.

"It's all a scam," Michael said.

"What?" I asked.

"School," he said.

"Yeah, I do know a lot of very educated Best Buy employees," I told him. He slapped me on the back hard again.

"As soon as the government started paying for it, all of these schools became unaccountable. It was better quality and less expensive before the government started paying for it. The government is literally the problem for everything—not the solution—and that's all you need to know. After that, the rest will all start to make sense," he explained. I scrunched up my face in disagreement but was trying to be polite and understand.

"You know it was kind of cool being a socialist back in San Francisco, but now the whole country is socialist," I said. Michael nodded his head in agreement.

"Yeah right, socialism. Everyone points to these tiny countries with homogeneous societies that pay for everything in Europe. Just remember this, America's population is 330 million, the annual taxes we collected last year was 3.7 trillion. Take a look at what the Democrats are proposing, the cost is upwards of fifty trillion! You know what would happen if the government turned on *that* amount of taxes?!...The whole country would begin to starve to death," he said. It was exactly like hearing the time my girlfriend in high school cheated on me. When someone tells you the truth, you recognize it, however when you are deeply invested, you never want to accept it. All of it was so simple but so hard to come to terms with. But I still couldn't believe that what he just said was the truth.

There's no way he just rattled off the death of my perception of reality. "Wait a second, no waaaay! We are the richest country in the world though!" I loudly told him.

Michael put his hand on my shoulder, "Roland, I'm telling you. It's basic math, man. It's not possible to pay for all of this." Even though I began to have my doubts the last few months, I still just couldn't fathom he was telling me the truth. I looked away from him, around at our surroundings, to focus on anything other than what was right in front of me. A storm began brewing inside me as I locked eyes with him.

"So Bernie Sanders is lying then?" I asked.

"No, he's not lying—he just doesn't know," Michael said. I took his hand off my shoulder as I was getting riled up now.

"Okay, that's insane! How could Bernie Sanders *not* know?! He's a US Senator!" I said.

"Roland, all you have to do is start making sense of the numbers he uses when he speaks," Michael said. I passionately pounded my chest.

"They make sense to me!" I screamed.

Michael tried to sympathize with me, "That's because you're still using your emotions to think and not your brain." *Did he just call me dumb?* My jaw dropped as I was immediately outraged.

"That's so ridiculous! Please! Please don't Ben Shapiro me right now!" I said loudly.

Michael looked at me as if he talked to a kid who just saw his pet die: "You're the one who asked for help," he told me, sympathetically. I put my hands on my waist like a toddler fed up with being told he has to clean his room.

"Well, maybe I don't want help from someone like you!" I said angrily. Michael paused and, in an instant, he tossed his hands up, "Whatever." And then Michael instantly began to walk away quickly, as he still had that "punk rock, I-don't-give-a-shit attitude." I sighed as I saw that I pissed off one of the only rational people I knew in California.

"Wait!" I screamed out. I run up beside him and begin walking next to him, as he kept his head down and didn't look at me.

"Every liberal has an ideology that they cling to—some can let it go when they see the facts, but some can't," he said.

"But how is what I believe an ideology?" I asked. Michael stopped on a dime, turned, and looked directly into my eyes.

"Because it's not based on fact; it's based on emotion. The stuff you believe can easily be debunked by just pulling out your phone; it is the same with everything they now believe. It's been at your fingertips the whole time. But if you want to know the *real* truth, the real truth is—well, you don't want to know the truth, and that's why me being here is a mistake," he said as he began to walk away from me again. I knelt over and began to feel sick, because what he's saying makes a whole lot of sense, and it's been a sense in my life that has been lacking since the day I got to California.

I stood up and yelled, "That's not true! I do want to know the truth!"

Surprisingly he stopped, turned around, and flopped his arms up in the air. "Fantastic! Then pull out your phone and search the cost of Universal Healthcare," he said. I very slowly pulled my phone from my pocket.

"Okay, no problem, let's see here..." I pulled up Google on my phone, and I saw the big different colored logo staring at me. "But you know what, Google is a huge corporation that makes billions of dollars. Obviously, Google isn't going to tell the truth—I mean right?!" I asked.

Michael laughed, "You think Google has a conservative conspiracy against you?! For fuck's sake you are worse off than I thought!" Michael began to walk away again but faster this time. I knew I couldn't let him go; I couldn't keep living in this crazy California Democrat nightmare where everything is racist and socialism is the answer to everything. I ran as fast as I could to catch him and grab onto his arm to stop him. I'm out of shape and out of breath.

"Ok. Ok. Ok. I believe you," I panted.

Michael paused, looking at me huffing for air and sighed. "No. You don't. But I want to help you, so why don't we start with the stuff *you do know* is a lie and work our way back." I took a moment to catch my breath. I prepared myself for the fact that I was probably not going to like any of this. I then stood up to look at him and nod in agreement. We turned back around towards the high-rise building with a club and begin walking.

"You mean like global warming?" I asked.

Michael says relieved, "Good, that's a start!" *I' m still out of breath.*

"Why doesn't anyone ever talk about the cost of things?" I asked.

"Because they are like you, blinded by an ideology. There is a place where they *do* talk about those things, but you aren't going to like it at first," he explained. I'm confused a little. I'm not really sure what he means by that, as I've never heard of any place that ever talked about government spending.

"What place?" I asked.

Fox News

I picked up my girlfriend from the club and we went back to the hotel, where she went to our room and fell asleep. Michael and I started drinking on the couch in the living room, and that's when he turned on the TV. Michael looked at the TV guide for a few minutes trying to find something. Suddenly I saw the red, white, and blue color scheme, with the American flag background that I had always learned to hate. It was about three a.m. in the morning on the West Coast, and there it was: Donald Trump's favorite TV show *Fox and Friends*. "Oh no, I can't watch this!" I said.

Michael smiled and asked, "Why not?" I pointed at the television like it had AIDS.

"It's Fox News! Our eyes will melt out of our heads!" I answered.

"I bet you've never watched Fox News in your life!" he said. *Duh!*

"Well, you'd be right, but..." Michael is perturbed.

"But what? Do you even know why liberals hate this channel?" he asked. I thought about it for a bit and couldn't think of anything.

"Because...because it's Fox News!" I explained loudly.

"And do you even know why *you* hate the channel?" Michael asked. I get frustrated because I can't think of an answer. I couldn't seem to understand or express why I don't like it, which was strange to me. I began to get very irritated at the thought of a hot conservative blonde woman calling me a "snowflake."

"Because...because it's Fox News, alright?! I shouldn't have to explain to you why I don't want to watch this!" I said.

Michael sighed, "Ok, why do you think *you* hate Fox News so much?!" he asked. I kept trying to think of an answer, but honestly, I didn't have one. My whole life, I was always told that Fox News was bad, evil, and conservative propaganda for poor dumb hillbillies. All I knew was that it was Republican, and Republicans were greedy and bad. In these strange times, where up was down and down was up, was Fox News *not* the evil TV channel I thought it was the whole time? There was no way this was true. It couldn't be.

But as I calmed down and watched Fox News over the next hour or so, as Michael and I drank, I noticed something: They seemed to be far saner than what I had seen on CNN or any of the other mainstream news channels. The other channels were obsessed with racism and socialism the last two years. I liked the socialism part but hated the obsession with racism, and it didn't make sense why these two issues were constantly connected. My whole life I was told how horrible Fox News was, and here they were making more sense than what I had always considered real news like CNN.

Fox News didn't talk about racism or sexism or spending money on universal government programs every two minutes. Fox News didn't make Republicans out to be some kind of old, grey monsters either. It was strange for me to get a glimpse of this other world that CNN always told me to hate. "You know why Fox News first came out?" Michael asked.

"No. Why?" I asked. "Back in the eighties when Ronald Reagan was elected, mainstream media treated him almost as badly as they are treating Donald Trump now." I looked over at Michael completely enamored.

"I had always heard from my parents that Reagan was a horrible president," Michael smiled. "Conservatives judge our presidents by how liberals and the mainstream news hate him." *Oh wow.*

"So he was one of the best then?" I asked.

Michael laughed, "A lot of people would agree with that." Michael then showed me clips of other right wing or alternative media, like Steven Crowder, Tim Pool, Ben Shapiro, Sargon of Akkad, Jordan Peterson, Dave Rubin. They all used these things I never heard of in California: facts and logic. They were all very good and obviously made more sense than anything in mainstream news, but the one that stood out the most was when Michael showed me clips of Tucker Carlson from Fox News. Finally someone who had his finger on the button of what was going on in crazy America the past year. Tucker Carlson had the coolest, most truthful motto ever for his show: "The sworn enemy of pomposity, smugness, and groupthink." *That was exactly it!*

I immediately started googling Tucker Carlson and wasn't shocked to find that he was hated—badly—by every liberal under the sun. They called him a white supremacist when it was obvious within the two minutes of watching him that he was a classical liberal, in the sense that he thought the unthinkable, horrible thought that everyone should be treated equally, including white people. That also meant no special treatment for anyone else. It was obvious why Democrats hated him; they saw the same thing I did: the truth. Democrats were so out of touch and deranged about what had happened in the election of 2016 that they were foaming at the mouth. Tucker told Democrats it wasn't Russia, racism, or sexism; it was *them* who caused Donald Trump. He was a 100% accurate. Michael fell asleep on the couch, but I didn't. I kept watching all of the YouTube channels he showed me, and I kept watching clips of Tucker Carlson. It was beginning to make more sense; however I just still couldn't understand the illogical obsession with racism and socialism. Those two connected didn't make sense to me.

A few hours later, I began watching one YouTube channel that he recommended, which had a documentary on Mao's Communist Cultural Revolution on it. Everything that was happening to the people of China was strikingly similar to what was happening here in America. There were brainwashed protesters and then there were rational people trying to make sense of why they were so mad. At about eleven in the morning, Hong and I gave Michael a hug and a thank you, as he groggily walked out the door. But before he did, I told him, "I still don't understand all the shit they are saying about white people."

Michael groggily turned around in the doorway and nonchalantly said, "Oh that's because *you are* the bourgeoisie now."

I leaned into the doorway. "What?" I asked curiously.

He answered, "For the last sixty years in America they tried to unite the poor against the rich; but that didn't work because in America we've always had a strong middle class. So Obama and his socialist friends in the media, like Bill Ayers, flipped it. Now they were trying to unite skin color versus European people, which is why they use the term 'people of color' now." I stood there in the doorway and it was like a cannonball just hit my stomach. *He's right. I didn't realize it before but now I do.* All the rhetoric about white privilege, white supremacy, cultural appropriation, and so on. I was now the bourgeoisie because of the socialist Democrats flipped ideology to incite revolution or, at the very least, vote for a Democratic Revolution.

What I had hated all my life was now turned against me. Now I was the bourgeoisie, and it was because of the color of my skin. It was *racism*. It was what liberals had said they were always against this whole time. Michael yawned and groggily waved goodbye, not realizing my whole world had been flipped upside down. As he walked down the hallway, I remembered why they use to call him possum. He would lay in the middle of the dorm hallways and pretend to be dead, until someone came up for him to scare. "Call me later," he said, as I stepped out of the hotel room to watch him leave with total shock at what he just told me. That was it! I couldn't believe it. But that *was* it! I instantly remembered Obama's portrait artist who had painted a Black woman cutting off a white woman's head.

And then of course I remembered Jeremiah Wright, Barack Obama's pastor from all those years ago, and all of the hateful and racist things he had said. I remembered how the media disregarded it, just like Obama's portrait artist, and acted like it was no big deal. It was exactly how they acted with Hillary's scandals. I also remembered believing the media was correct at the time and that it was no big deal that a presidential candidate had a pastor who hated America and white people. *How could I have been so stupid?*

My mouth and eyes were wide open while I was standing in the middle of the hotel hallway watching Michael leave my sight when he got into the elevator. I was flabbergasted but immediately jolted back to reality when my girlfriend Hong yelled from inside our hotel room. "Baby! Time to take shower and get dressed!" I couldn't move but could respond somehow.

"Uhhh. Okay, I'm coming!" I called. I walked back into the hotel room and shut the door. I was out of it, but somehow remembered to not forget anything from the hotel room.

We left to go back to Los Angeles a few hours later and, to the dismay of all the cars on the five freeway, I let my girlfriend Hong drive. She was giggling as she swerved through two lanes into the carpool lane, and that was when she noticed my eyes getting watery. "Baby, are you crying?!" she asked.

"No. I have something in my eyes." I told her. That wasn't true of course. The reason I was trying to hold back my tears was because I was looking at my phone and viewing the link that Michael texted me. America was twenty-two trillion in debt and the Democrats wanted to add forty-five trillion to that number. Universal Healthcare for 330 million Americans would cost 4.5 trillion. A Universal Basic Income would cost 3.5 trillion. The richest man in America only had 86 billion. If the government took—not taxed—but *took* all of the money of the ten richest men in America, it would only amount to 400 billion. There was no one percent who was going to pay for all of this with higher taxes. *That was a lie.* It was me and everyone else who would pay for it.

He then sent me a link to the total amount of wealth that all the billionaires in America had. Out of 540 total billionaires, the total wealth those billionaires had amounted to 2.6 trillion dollars. 2.6 trillion dollars wasn't even close to 3.5 trillion needed a year for Universal Basic Income, or 4.5 trillion needed for Universal Healthcare, or any of the socialist programs Democrats wanted. I then viewed the welfare statistics. It was obvious to see who was struggling and who wasn't, and instead of helping these minority communities, Democrats were telling them that white people had everything handed to them because of white privilege, so there was no point in even trying. Democrats were telling them that they had to work harder to achieve what white people achieved, so they might as well give up.

America had been running the biggest poverty program in the history of the world, while Democrats were telling the very same people using it that it was their skin color holding them back. *This was disgusting.* I had been lied to my whole life and was told that socialism would help people. Democrats didn't want socialism to help anyone; they wanted socialism for more power and more votes. I was a living conservative meme. I was an economic illiterate with a master's degree in Fine Art who had been duped by years and years of propaganda since the day I was born. It was in this moment that I realized I was a snowflake. I eventually couldn't hold myself back. I wept and made that silly little noise everyone makes when they can no longer hold back unbelievable sadness. "Baby! What happened?!" Hong asked. I didn't know how to tell her.

"Nothing. Don't worry about it," I explained as my face made that awful crying noise. I had been lied to my entire life. All the movies, music, news, TV shows, and all those years of schooling had all been lies. Everything my whole life that had shaped and formed my opinion, from history, to economics, to immigration, to race, all of it was one lie after another. A bomb had exploded in my mind, and it was like all the chains that had been wrapped around it had been set free. I spent all those years being angry at the world and hating and blaming America. All those years I spent hating and blaming capitalism. All those years spent blaming corporations and billionaires. All those years I spent wanting an equal and fairer society. *It was all bullshit.* The crying became even more uncontrollable. I was crying like a kid whose goldfish just died.

Hong pulled off the freeway and into a gas station. "Baby, I gonna get you tissue and water," Hong told me loudly. She shut the door and ran as I sat in the car alone. I scrolled through my phone and saw one anti-Trump media article after another. It was all bullshit and I knew it now. It was all a charade so they could keep up the dog and pony show. Trump was a threat to all the BS they created for sixty years. I didn't utter a word for the two-hour drive back to Los Angeles, as poor Hong sat there and worried. The first thing I did when I got home, after putting away my luggage and wiping away my tears, was record the Tucker Carlson show for everyday of the week. The only thing more Republican I could do was start wearing khakis and join a golf club. I couldn't believe that Republicans, of all people, were right the whole time. Tucker Carlson was a breath of fresh air from a world that had gone mad. As I'm setting everything up on my TV remote, I noticed my phone on my bed vibrating. It was my hippie mom from Indiana. I had an inclination on who and what it was about but hoped to be wrong.

My Sister Janet and Her Trump Derangement Syndrome

Somewhere within the first two years of Trump being president, I had noticed my sister Janet post a meme from the Democratic Socialists of America group on Facebook. It was one I had seen posted before, but the one I had seen had a DSA label at the bottom, whereas the one my sister posted was without it. It was a pyramid of white supremacy, and at the bottom of the pyramid was making a joke, while at the top of the pyramid was black genocide. Somehow this was the new logic of the communist infiltrated Democratic Party. White men were now the bourgeoisie; I was the oppressor. If I told a joke, it could leave a whole continent extinct. I also had white male privilege, and no one could compete with me in society because my skin was magical. *Who were the racists again?!* It was no longer rich billionaires or corporations versus the working class like Karl Marx had hypothesized in *The Communist Manifesto*, it was me and my white male skin. They had flipped the prism of oppression. It was no longer Karl Marx, and his theory, but now Moses Hess.

Regardless of what was in my bank account or how much power I actually had; I was the bad guy. If you are a white male like me, then you are responsible for all the evils of the world. I knew in my heart that I wasn't the evil doer, racist, or oppressive, and I was never handed anything because I was white, but these people were now brainwashed to believe otherwise. I began to understand my own flaws in thinking with this oppressor versus oppressed logic. I had blamed corporations and these imaginary evil billionaires, or as Bernie Sanders called it, "The one percent," for every problem in the world, for almost my entire adult life. But now I was the problem, as it had been turned around against me. These people who were blaming me for all their problems didn't know who I was, and I didn't know who this mysterious invisible one percent was, who in my mind used to be supposedly destroying society.

My sister was a mother of two interracial kids, and if she truly believed that white men telling a joke led to Black genocide, she might be harder to save than I was. Ironically though, I had a sneaking suspicion that both of her children were closeted Trump supporters. They both rode ATVs, had an affinity for hunting, and liked a lot of right-wing profiles on Facebook. They probably knew I was an ungrateful snowflake like their mother was this whole time. As I was beginning to come to terms with all these new realizations, I still couldn't say I was quite saved yet. It was all still just too unreal. How could I have been lied to by the Democrats this entire time? Or maybe it wasn't that I was lied to, but that the liberal overlords on television were the dumb ones instead of the smart ones all along. It made sense.

The people I worked with in Hollywood were not smart, and the people who called themselves journalists were somehow even dumber. Artsy people in California were abstract thinkers and, the more I thought about it, I had been an abstract thinker too. Putting too much of us in one state together is a *bad idea!* And it's an even worse idea to give that state too much political influence over the rest of the country via the television. However even with my "woke" thinking, I was still smart enough to see the BS the last few years. Maybe for some reason the propaganda never fully kept its hold on me. But still, how could the conservative hillbillies and rednecks I grew up with in Indiana be smarter than I was? How were they right all along about politics? Capitalism and freedom were so simple, and yet it had been the answer all along. I had trusted the mainstream news media, Hollywood, and the Democrats for far too long. I was beginning to understand what Trump meant by fake news, although I had seen plenty of it for the past two years and should have known or realized what he was talking about then.

When I got that phone call from my mother, I had an inclination it was about my sister and her "wokeness." I had forgotten during the Obama years that my sister became some sort of rabid Black Lives Matter supporter who hated police. She even styled her hair to have cornrows and used a ton of self-tanner. At the time I never thought anything of it. *Jesus, I hope no one has any pictures of me in San Francisco at anti-Bush rallies.* At the urgent request of my mother, and her threat that she would sell all of my vintage GI Joes, which is my only plan for retirement, I bought a seven-hundred-dollar plane ticket back to Indiana immediately. Something was up, and it wasn't good. I left from the LAX airport the next morning and arrived in Indianapolis by evening. I cursed the whole way.

My mother, who looks like a time capsule from the hippie sixties, picked me up in her refurbished 1977 Volkswagen van. We began driving down the long highway home, with nothing but pasture and snow in our view. She was quiet most of the way, until I asked her what this whole thing was about. She replied very calmly, "Your sister was racially profiled by a police officer." *Oh my god!*

"What the...." I was stunned. "....who would do such a thing?!" I asked. I began sweating and frantically thinking, *Maybe the world was reverted back to the racist nineteen twenties!* Maybe it was I who was the *only* one who didn't see it. Maybe it was I who was too ignorant to see the truth *all* along. But then I suddenly remembered something important. "Wait, Janet is white, so how could she be racially profiled?" I asked.

My mother's eyes wandered around nervously, trying to come up with an answer. "This whole thing is Trump's fault! If Trump hadn't colluded with Russia, your sister would be fine!" my mother screamed. I tilted my head like a puppy does when filled with curiosity.

"What do you mean this is Trump's fault?" I cautiously asked, hoping I hadn't just bought a seven-hundred-dollar plane ticket because of delusions of my self-tanning sister. We soon arrived at my sister's brick and mortar house that was out in the middle of nowhere. I let my mother walk in first, but then I walked into my sister's quaint little house, where I saw something I wasn't expecting. Amongst the gaudy African-themed decor of her Indiana home was my Afro-haired sister Janet spinning around in her nightgown; she was going off on some sort of inconsolable rant. Her two college-aged kids, Brandon and Tatum, plus my flower child mother were trying to calm her.

"This wall was created by white men! This sofa was created by white men! This TV was created by white men!" she said as she spun out of control like a helicopter in Somalia. I was frozen, as I thought I had seen the worst of Trump Derangement Syndrome in Los Angeles. However I saw that my sister's TV was Sony.

"Actually no, the TV is Sony...." I told her matter-of-factly. Janet stopped on a dime and looks right at me, with eyes that could pierce a tank. My mother and nephews all stopped trying to control her and looked at me as well. "It was made in a factory in Mexico," I told them happily and ignorantly, as I felt like I've subdued the situation. Everyone was silent. Brandon adjusted his John Deere hat while Tatum relaxed his tense shoulders. My sister raised her hands with long nails like an eagle. She gritted her teeth together like an animal. Her eyebrows formed triangles of anger.

She let out a giant holler, "Trump Suppoooorteeerrr!"

I blurted out, "Oh shit!" I ducked quickly as she flew right over me like an all-pro linebacker. I heard a loud thud as she toppled over a lamp, blacking out the lightbulb, and hitting the wall behind me. My nephews Brandon and Tatum ran up to see if she was okay. I stood up and looked down at her and saw that she was completely knocked out. Her Afro-headed hair bashed into the wall behind me, leaving an indentation. We almost called 911 but the last thing we wanted was to alert the local police, which was like Satan's little helpers to her.

As my sister Janet was helped upstairs to take a nap, I ordered pizza and turned on the living room television. I had noticed that the channel that was left on was MSNBC. I had always watched CNN because it was tamer. I had seen clips of pseudo-intellectuals screaming about racism on MSNBC, and I knew I could never handle two minutes of that channel. A few hours later, after watching an episode of Al Sharpton's show on MSNBC, I somehow resisted the urge to hang myself to atone for all my white man sins; I prepared to talk to my so-called progressive sister Janet. She was calmed down now, and sat on her couch with an ice packet on her head. I sat across from her and relaxed in the old rocking chair that my mother gave my sister years ago. As she came to, I built up the courage to try and reason with her.

"Maybe America isn't as greedy and evil as I thought it was, and maybe America isn't as racist as you thought it was," I said. Immediately my bronzed, self-tanned sister steamed with anger.

"Orrrr!...maybe you're a racist too!" she yelled. I couldn't help but roll my eyes, despite the fear of being karate chopped.

"Uhhhh no...I'm not," I told her. She took off her ice packet and stood up with conviction as she pointed her finger at me.

"Yes! That's it! You're a racist!" she proclaimed. She was getting herself worked up again; I could see it by the way she was grinding her teeth. Tatum stopped playing video games on his computer in the corner, and Brandon ran in from the kitchen holding a cold piece of pizza. Our mother stood up from the couch very slowly. I stayed calm and slowly stood up as well, but with my hands out, ready to catch Kung Fu from a delusional Hillary supporter and MSNBC watcher. But then I thought of something clever. Everyone in the room could see it as I smirked. Everyone paused and waited, but they also gave me that look that says, "Please don't."

"Actually, have you ever thought that maybe...*you* are the racist?" I asked. Both of her interracial kids bent their neck to look on at me with curiosity, which was the same way I did at their grandmother in her van. Suddenly Janet's eyes began blinking intensely, and very slowly she dropped her hand from pointing at me, as if *all* her energy slowly began to drain out of her body. Her head then slowly dropped as well, as her whole body turned to her left; she looked into the mirror on the wall by the coat racket. Janet's head raised and she saw herself in the reflection. "I'm...I'm the racist?" she asked.

Brandon, my sister Janet's first son, smiled with excitement from the hallway. "Hold on, I have to get my phone so I can record this!" Brandon flopped his pizza on a nearby table and jetted out of the living room faster than I ever saw. Tatum giggled and went back to playing video games on the computer in the corner. I walked over and stood next to my sister as she looked in the mirror.

"Yes...you see...when you assume something about a whole race of people you never met, like that they have privilege, that's actually racist..." Janet looked on with surprise.

"You mean..." she almost replied as I interrupted her.

"Yes...there are Black people who are *not* oppressed," I told her.

"Really?!" Janet asked with joy.

"In Los Angeles there are tons of Black movie executives, TV writers, bankers, models, business owners. Did you know that there are actually three hundred thousand Black millionaires in America?!" I asked.

"Really?! That many?!" Janet enthusiastically asked.

"Oh yes, that many!" I replied with a smile on my face.

"Why have I not heard about this?" she asked. I thought about it for a bit.

"Well Janet, you're blinded by an ideology. Also you've never left Indiana before, and you watch *a hell of a lot of MSNBC.*" I said. Janet paused but then turned to me and grabbed me by the shoulders.

"That's it!...Indiana has too many white men, and it must be destroyed!" she said with glee. I frowned.

"Uhhh, no," I told her.

"What do you mean no, you fascist?!" my sister said as her teeth began to grind again.

"Because killing white people is *also* racist," I replied.

"Are you sure?!" Janet asked with just as much excitement back. I pretended to ponder the question for a bit.

"I'm pretty sure," I said. Tatum stood up from his computer desk and pointed at me in a very pissed-off way.

"If you redpill mom before she pays my speeding ticket, I'll kill you," Tatum said. I shushed him with my finger as Janet focused on me instead of Tatum.

"Then what's the solution?!" my sister asked in all sincerity. I pondered the question for a bit, but then it hit me. It was so obvious. It was the same problem our American culture has had for decades now. This wasn't classical liberalism in our culture coming from the TV; it was Moses Hess disguised as liberalism. My feminist neighbor Goldie blamed the patriarchy and men for her problems. The anti-racists like my friend Augusta and my sister Janet blamed white people for their problems. My Hispanic friend Juan and illegal friend Manuel (he should be deported) blamed America and its history, and for even existing for their problems. And the original hippie Marxists like myself and my mother, blamed billionaires and corporations.

It was so obvious to see, yet I hadn't totally got it until standing there in front of my lunatic Afro-headed sister. My eyes blew up with excitement as Janet anticipated an answer. "*I got it!* The solution is to...treat all citizens of the United States as individuals...equally!" I said. Janet stood still and was not thrilled by the solution. Her face discombobulated as she contemplated the notion and then walked away from me to the center of the living room.

"To treat everyone as individuals? Equally?!" She asked. I clapped my hands together in excitement.

"Yes!" I said.

"But what about all the rich people and...the corporations you hate?" Janet asked.

"We should treat them equally too!" I said. Janet almost fell backwards. Then she put her hand over her mouth and gasped.

"Oh my god! What's wrong with you?!" Janet asked. I paused thinking about it for a bit. An excitement came over me. I clapped my hands together again.

"I've changed!" I proclaimed so all the world could hear.

Janet gasped again, "You've changed?!" I sat down on the arm of a chair across from her.

"Yeah! It's great! You should *really, really* try it," I told her. Janet squinted her eyes as she thought about this strange notion. Brandon ran back into the room with his iPhone pointed at both of us.

"Ok! Now go back to the part where Mom is asking herself in the mirror if she's a racist!" Brandon said. The room got quiet and we all just sat still for a while. She was quite normal for the next few days and eventually went back to work. And apparently no one had been racially profiled by the police at all, despite my Caucasian sister Janet's insistence they had. My sister had a taillight out, which took me almost a whole day to figure out how to put a new one in. When I prepared to leave for Los Angeles on a red eye, I noticed my sister Janet watching CNN before I took my luggage out of her house. I had ordered her cable company to turn off all the news channels but they still hadn't gotten rid of CNN. Apparently, they don't consider it a news channel either.

I sighed as the Uber driver put my luggage into his trunk. I hugged my hippie mother goodbye, as I realized that my sister Janet wasn't ready for the Fox News conversation yet. I got in the Uber car and tried to forget all about it. I hopped on the plane back to Los Angeles that night, hoping that Don Lemon wouldn't continue to regress my so-called progressive sister. I wasn't entirely positive about the situation, but I tried to think about something else anyway. What began bothering me even more was how I was going to tell everyone in Los Angeles that I was now a Trump-supporting Republican. Being quiet about who I was has never really been a part of my nature.

Parkland School Shooting

The holidays went by in Los Angeles with protests and hatred for Donald Trump still everywhere. The biggest nonpolitical story by February was the Tide Pod Challenge. Kids were eating Tide Pods and dying on YouTube. This seemed to fit the strange times, but it was about to get stranger. America is a country that has always loved its guns. I was never really a part of that circle when I grew up in Indiana, but I understood it. I had always known the importance of it. There had been a phrase in America for as long as I can remember, and the phrase goes "Guns don't kill people, people kill people." It's about as simple as one can understand, however these weren't simple times. Now that Donald Trump was president, everything was up for debate. If Donald Trump tweeted that he liked fresh water, an environmentalist might just write a news article about how fresh water was racist. If Donald Trump tweeted french fries weren't healthy, then a nutritionist would come out in support of eating french fries to stop racism. If Donald Trump tweeted an NBA basketball player hit a nice jump shot, CNN might have a political commentator come on and talk for an hour about how Trump is sexist for mentioning the NBA instead of the WNBA.

The goal was to make Donald Trump look bad in any way possible. The more disturbing part was that people were actually buying it. Donald Trump was *still* the center of everyone's conversations, and he had been for one year and three months now. I wondered how this man could take such a beating and keep going. It was February 2018, and it was the third Valentine's Day with Hong, which was the longest I had ever been with anyone. We went to the Palm's Pacific Hotel, where we had our first date, and drank by the fire out on the patio overlooking Los Angeles. That's when I received the best Valentines present anyone could have ever given me. It was a card that one of her English-speaking friends must have written for her. It said, "Baby, I love you, and just want you to know that on November 4, 2016, I voted for Donald Trump."

I looked up from the card instantly and began beaming with happiness. I was blown away. My mouth dropped and my eyes got huge as I looked at the most beautiful woman in the world. My Cambodian mama Hong was based and redpilled the whole time. "Are you serious?! This is amazing! Why didn't you tell me?!"

Hong got very serious and stared at me, "Baby, you know why." I laughed.

"Holy shit! You're right! I would have had a heart attack if you told me then. But yeah! This is amazing! I'm so happy!" Hong looked at me empathetically.

"You know I from Cambodia. Socialism not good baby."

I smiled, "Well fuck, I know now! Jesus, you know...I remember one time I woke up and could have sworn you were on The Donald on Reddit. I thought I was dreaming." Hong smirked and pointed her finger at me.

"Top Kek, baby!" I laughed so hard again. Kekistan was a fictional nation made up by conservatives who trolled liberals about their obsession with racism. My girlfriend was a Kekistani troll this whole time, who had probably been trolling liberals with "It's okay to be white" memes. Meanwhile, this whole time, I was a delusional economic illiterate socialist Democrat who she was probably praying would soon learn math. I was so ecstatic that I could barely contain myself.

"I cannot fucking believe this!" I blurted out. She put her finger to her mouth and shushed me quietly.

"Don't say too loud, baby." I quieted down and leaned forward as everyone looked at us; Hong looked very serious. "Remember, lots of people just like you before. Don't talk too much. Don't say too much. Same happen in Cambodia when socialism came. No one allow to say anything to the people," she said. I looked at Hong and realized how serious this all is to her, and how it should have been to me a long time ago.

"What can we do?" I asked as Hong sipped her tea.

"Be happy they do not take guns yet," she answered. I looked at Hong and realized she was a treasure of knowledge this whole time. It was interesting, however, what we woke up to the next day—a school shooting at Parkland High School in Florida. It happened on Valentine's Day, and just like the Charlottesville thing, no one really cared because the socialist mainstream media hadn't had time to pump up the volume yet. We had many school shootings since Columbine about twenty years ago, but of course just like the Charlottesville pseudo-event, this one was different because Donald Trump was president. Donald Trump liked America, capitalism, and of course the right to bear arms. The media despised him, so you must despise him too.

You had to follow what the media said because you wouldn't want to think differently than everyone else, right? Thinking differently was of course a bad thing now to liberals. If CNN said that shit sandwiches cured racism, well you better get that shit sandwich in your mouth, bitch. Not only that, but if you dared to question shit sandwiches in public or on social media you would be immediately met with brainwashed zombies who were hysterical at you for daring to question the liberal propaganda machine. This was the free country with free speech everyone now lived in. *Or was it becoming the socialist country my girlfriend escaped from?* I was starting to understand what Donald Trump meant by saying, "Make America Great Again."

What happened next, I likened to a mixture of the attention-craving culture our society had cultivated, and the liberal socialism of the nineteen sixties, converging within the fourth generation of youth that it got its hands on. After the school shooting, we began seeing videos of a bald Latina girl on social media everywhere. We also saw videos of a scrawny metrosexual-looking kid as well. These two people were Emma González and David Hogg. The first video everyone saw was of Emma González's bald head at a press conference, where she was whining and crying in a way that was meant to look revolutionary but instead seemed very inauthentic. When I worked in Hollywood, I saw this a lot. She probably saw this as her big break. David Hogg was next, and he seemed to be calmer and more collected, more politician minded than the typical teenage kid, but he was just as dumb as the bald Latina girl. Yet he probably saw this as his big break into fame as well. It was if they instinctively knew what to do. They knew the world was watching, the media hated Donald Trump, and his supporters love the constitution and the freedom to own guns. They also knew CNN and the liberal media would cover the shit out of this if they blamed Trump, America, and guns.

It was the perfect way for them to gain social media followers, which is ultimately every American teens' dream now. The teenagers of America were trained to be reality TV and internet stars, and it was our culture that had taught them exactly how to do it. They had been brainwashed just like everyone else to believe that Trump was the Anti-Christ of the world, and that anything that happened in America or around the world, was his fault, America's fault, and capitalism's fault. And so it began. Interview after interview for two months was wall to wall coverage on Emma González and David Hogg, saying the most asinine things. We were also presented with the cringiest of cringy magazine covers. One of the magazine covers had all these kids with their fists in the air, looking like wannabe Che Guevara. It was hilarious!

However if you looked on social media, and on television, people were still actually buying this garbage. The media went ape shit for these kids. The truth was that we had already seen what happened to countries who had banned guns throughout history. Hong lived under Pol Pot's socialism and she was right; we did not want to fucking ban guns in this country! This was another sign of our enormously funded government education system not working. Or perhaps it was working, as somehow every high school kid was socialist now. Britain banned guns in the 90s, and now they are trying to ban knives. What's more hilarious about this is that Britain banning guns had no effect on people being shot whatsoever. The statistics stayed the same. What we did see however, is more control from the government surrounding speech.

Britain has very unusual hate speech laws. Britain once threw a journalist in jail for speaking against Islamic gang rapes. Britain threw a comedian in jail for teaching his girlfriend's pug, as a joke, to Heil Hitler. Then of course we have all the countries across the world who banned guns right before socialism took hold of their country; those people then starved and were killed in the millions. Now suddenly, with half the country wanting Bernie Sanders-style socialism, they were also chomping at the bit to ban guns because of a few teenagers on TV. It was like living in some really bad predictable movie. This went on and on and I got really sick of seeing these two kids' faces. I didn't have any guns but just seeing these two dumb kids made me want to buy an AR-15. We all seemed to know more than we really did when we are teenagers; now just imagine CNN putting a camera on you at seventeen and telling you that everything you believe is right. It's a winning bet that it would have made for some hysterical moments. Except the only people who seemed to be doing any laughing were logical and rational people, otherwise known as conservatives.

I had joined The Donald on Reddit like my girlfriend. Finally I was meeting people who weren't Los Angeles liberal insane. A liberal I knew in the film industry posted on Facebook about how he knew these kids were sent from God to tell us all how to live. He had one hundred likes. I hadn't bought a gun yet, but I was making sure my doors were locked more often. The levels of insanity were reaching all-time highs, and that wasn't even mentioning the fact that some of the kids who advocated for wanting to ban guns were also eating Tide Pods. CNN then had a town hall in Florida, the state where the school shooting happened. They had Dana Loesch, the spokesperson of the NRA, speak to the audience with the now famous children who were advocating for the banning of guns. The whole event rivaled a medieval public execution.

The town hall of people yelled, booed, and hissed at Dana Loesch and the NRA. Emma González, David Hogg, and Cameron Kasky called the NRA a terrorist organization and the crowd cheered. The NRA had two million American members in it, and here these kids were who don't know anything calling all of them terrorists. The town hall was full of adults cheering these kids on like rabid animals. These kids seemed to be able to say anything, and no one was allowed to question them. If you dared to even hint of it on social media, the mob of social justice warriors would descend on you.

It was about 2 a.m. and I had just gotten back from a club in Los Angeles. I went on a tirade for whoever I could find posting anything moronic about banning guns. It was like taking all of my film industry contacts, burning them, and flushing them down the toilet. *I didn't care.* Nothing good in Hollywood has been made since the nineties. They all wanted to ban guns now because the TV news and social media told them it was a good idea. Hollywood was intellectually and creatively bankrupt; it had been for years and I was just fooling myself that it would ever go back to the golden age of film. California, a place that used to be a place of free and open thinking, was now a place of conformity. A camera operator I worked with posted to social media, "If we could all just come together and end the gun violence together by turning in all handguns, rifles, and bullets, the world would be a better place." *Maybe if we chopped off all of our penises, we could end rape too.* I told him he was a whiny pussy and blocked him.

Then there was a music video producer I worked with. He posted to social media, "Owning a firearm is toxic masculinity unhinged. Be a human!" People were really buying into these pseudoscience theories and mixing them together with reasons to ban things or make things mandatory (all Democrat policies). I could not take it anymore. Los Angeles had become the city of letting everyone know how virtuous they were while telling the rest of the world that if they didn't give up their rights, they were bad people. For one week I went to the gun range and blasted every target they put in front of me. I had been in California for thirteen years, and I had changed, but these people had *really* changed. I didn't run my whole life by what CNN told me was good and evil, and I definitely didn't buy into all the fake narratives and pseudoscience they were coming up with. I hated the idea of being wrong all those years about socialism, but I hated whatever this was with these people who called themselves liberal–socialists more.

I was watching TV on my couch when Goldie, my favorite feminist neighbor, walked through the door and stood there pissed off. "What the fuck, dude?!" She said.

"What?" I asked.

"You know we can all see your political arguments on Facebook, don't you?" she asked.

"And?" I replied.

"Are *you* a fucking Trump supporter now?!" she asked as she boiled with intensity. I breathed in and out still not capable of saying it. I stayed silent as Goldie stood there with her hands on her hips staring at me. "Yo, *answer* the question!" she screamed.

I looked at Goldie and very slowly and calmly said, "Yes. I'm a Trump supporter now."

"Oh my God, dude! Why don't you go back to the Midwest with all the other rednecks!" she screamed. I flipped through the channels on my TV as I pretended not to care.

"You know, that might be a good idea," I replied.

"Oh yeah?! Are you going to work in a fucking factory, Mr. American Slave?! Holy shit, you are the most contradictory person I've ever met!" she screamed.

"That's funny coming from a person who believes in peace and equality but who hates men and white people," I said.

"You fucking asshole!" she yelled.

"I see what you post on social media too," I replied. Goldie scoffed.

"Patriarchy has oppressed women for centuries, and acknowledging white privilege helps create a fairer and more equal society," she said as she sounded like she was reading a script.

"Telling black and brown people that we get everything free because of our skin color? Yeah, I don't think so," I told her. Goldie punched the door.

"You're such a dick!" she said as she walked out of the doorway, slamming my screen door behind her.

"There's no such thing as equality, Goldie!" I yelled, knowing that my newfound little nugget of truth would irk her like no other. I went to bed that night but woke up at about three a.m. to some noises and laughter of girls outside my window. Usually that would be something that excited me, however in this moment I knew better. I turned on the front porch light and went out to the yard and didn't see anyone there. However I did see that my entire house was toilet papered. They had done a good job. They made sure the toilet paper was all over the roof and trees. I went to my door and saw that they had written in big red letters with red paint "Racist" on my wooden door.

I spent the next three hours taking down the toilet paper and washing off the red paint. I finished right at 6 a.m. before the rest of the neighborhood woke up to see it. The next day when I got home, I saw Goldie and Tanya outside on their porch laughing. I went into my garage and found the American flag that had been left behind from a tenant before me years ago. It was old and dusty, and I had never paid it any attention, putting boxes and tools on it the entire time. I shook off the dust and cleaned it off. For the first time in my life, I raised an American flag on my front lawn, as Goldie and Tanya were sitting on their porch, frozen with shock. Goldie stood up and took off her sunglasses with anger like I had never seen before. It was quite possibly the funniest thing I had ever seen. It was the first time I really realized how much liberals hated America. I had always fooled myself by telling myself when I was liberal that I only wanted to change America. That was just another lie. I might have never been as brainwashed as these people are now, but at one point I was definitely close, and I was happy to be waking up from it.

Three White Men Walk Into a Hollywood Talent Agency

There we were, three schlubs waiting for rewrite work in a room that looked like it was put together by Liberace. Since the recession of 2008, Hollywood never really got back on its feet as far as independent financing was concerned. Everything was superhero films now. However there were a ton of people looking to make movies in America, and places like these capitalized on it. Let's say some idiot calls up from a state most of Los Angeles has never heard of and says they wrote a screenplay and want this agency to make it into a movie. The operator on the phone passes it to a producer rep, then the producer rep acts very interested and says they just need to look at the screenplay first. When the producer rep eventually gets to it about two months down the road, they skim through it to find the name of the main character and the ending of the screenplay. Maybe they also find a few pieces of dialogue to talk about. They call up the aspiring screenwriter and say, "Wow, I love the screenplay!"

The aspiring screenwriter gets excited, because all of his dreams are coming true. The producer rep then tells the aspiring screenwriter the rub. For the low, low, low price of fourteen thousand dollars, they can hire a screenwriter to polish the screenplay and get it ready for the studios. That is usually when the aspiring screenwriter either hangs up or begins writing a fat check. This sounds like a scam, right? It's not. It's not a guarantee, but some of them get their screenplays optioned. A very small percentage make a career out of it and end up here with me. And an even lower percentage ever get a movie made—in fact, almost no one gets that. It's usually the most talented people who hang up the phone and usually the least talented who start writing the check. But a few of the ones who write that check have gone on to do some cool things. It has nothing to do with white privilege but don't tell an oppressed victim with three baby mamas that.

It's crazy how Hollywood ends up working. The office is right off of Rodeo Drive, a street that is so wealthy and clean that you could eat off the concrete. I was the youngest of the group in the office currently waiting at 32. I had met the other two guys before at this agency. Jeff was 55 years old, fat and balding, and dressed more like an accountant than a writer. Alan was 48 and lived in Venice Beach where hipster clothing was required. However, as usual, I had a hangover and looked like I just got out of bed. I had been coming to this place for work for five years, so at this point I didn't really care much. So there we were patiently waiting, when the assistant walked in. He was about twenty-five, metrosexual, flamboyantly gay, had a lisp, and a voice that could scare dogs away. "Sorry boys, but you know the drill; we need to hire more women of color this month."

Alan's head dropped, as this is something we heard a lot more the last few months. "I'm not sure Beyoncé is really interested in this type of work," Alan replied.

"Once we are at fifty percent, we'll call you," the intern said. I couldn't help it. I laughed out loud.

"They are trying to socially engineer hack writing!" I said.

In a mocking voice, Alan said, "Diversity makes us stronger!" The gay intern was instantly mad.

"You know what?! It's 2018! If you three white men don't like it, maybe you should find new careers!" the intern said. He then walked out flailing his hands all over the place like he just gay owned us.

"Looks like I'll be working Uber in the mornings," I said.

"Screw that. Let's get a drink instead," Alan replied.

"Orrr, we could get a drink and do Uber?" I suggested. It was about noon when we walked into a dive bar in Burbank. We got our drinks and sat outside on stools around a little tabletop.

"Trump becoming president is the worst thing that has ever happened to me," Jeff said.

I balked and said, "Oh, come on! As soon as things start getting stolen and people don't get to work on time, it will be back to choosing employment by merit." I smiled happily. However, Jeff didn't.

"Not true. Over at a studio my cousin works at, she says minorities have a thirty-minute grace period," Jeff said.

"Yeah and if things get stolen, it will be the perfect time to fire the white guy in the cubicle they don't like," Alan replied.

"They can't keep losing money for the sake of racial equality," I said.

"I've been thinking about getting a *real* job," Jeff said. I could barely believe it. "I had a good run but having to work on an African space opera and a drag queen cop movie last year has really taken its toll on me," Jeff said.

"It's just a phase," I replied.

"Think how bad it will be if he gets re-elected," Alan said. I scoffed again.

"More ban white people tweets and more protests," I replied.

"And more diversity needed on rewrite work," Jeff added in a concerned way.

"Maybe they will have proven they aren't racist by then," I replied.

"If it means not having to teach anymore, I'll vote for the Black transgender socialist who the Democrats put up," Alan said.

"And you don't think it will be worse once they put this stuff into law?" I asked.

"What law? They will be so happy that they don't have a white man as president that they will forget all about us," Alan said.

"I doubt it," I replied pessimistically.

"Not a chance," Jeff responded.

"The Black transgender president will hand out free money, and *all* will be peaceful in the world," Alan said gleefully.

"And your taxes will be 90%," I responded.

"And if I had a real job, I'd have to worry about that, now wouldn't I?" Alan said with a smile on his face.

"A very, very, solid point," Jeff said. I took a swig of my tequila and Diet Coke and saw David Hogg being interviewed by CNN on the outside bar television.

"Hey, have you guys thought about buying a gun?" I asked. Both looked up at the television, then looked at each other, and then looked at me like I was crazy. They said together, "You don't have one?!"

March For Our Lives Protest

It was Saturday March 24, 2018, and the media had talked about this protest for the last five weeks. Isn't the name of this little protest cute? It's the month of March, and these kids are marching for their lives, because it's just so dangerous out there in America. That was the message you were supposed to believe. David Hogg and Emma González were superstars now, even appearing on *The Ellen DeGeneres Show*. The media however was keeping everyone in the dark about several things, one of them being that Emma Gonzales was one of the people who tormented the shooter Nicholas Cruz every day. Someone actually brought this up and it received very little coverage because of course it didn't follow the liberal media narrative that these kids were victims. When it was brought up to Emma González, she made no apologies for this. She acted like Nicholas Cruz deserved to be tormented saying, "You didn't know this kid, we did."

It was more disgusting hypocrisy from the media and Democrats, but it wasn't anything new at this point. I continued to ask myself if it had always been this way, and my guess is that it probably had to some extent, but it was just more obvious because they were overplaying their hand on anti-Trump hate; they still seemed to think that the internet with different sources didn't exist. The day the March for Our Lives protest began, my girlfriend wanted to run errands in Chinatown. I tried to get out of it as I brushed my teeth realizing that today would be a bad day to fight traffic downtown. "Uhh, maybe we could go to Long Beach instead?" I suggested.

"To replace necklace? No! You said today! Must replace necklace today!" she said as she stomped her flat feet out of the bathroom, meaning that I had to do what she wanted or else. There we were in downtown Los Angeles, at a Chinese jewelry store, when hordes of people began walking by with their kids, all holding signs begging for Trump to take their rights away. They had called this guy Hitler for the last two years and were now epileptic for him to take away their right to defend themselves.

I walked out of the jewelry store because I had to see it for myself. Hong called for me to stay but I didn't listen. I stood in the middle of the street, with parents and their kids all walking past me, as they all were screaming for their rights to be taken in unison together. It was one of the most frightening feelings I've ever had. Hong looked on at me from inside the jewelry store, as we seemed to share a moment as all of this was happening. It was if we both knew what all of this meant one day if these people ever got their way. She was a lot stronger than I was. She went on about her day and never mentioned anything else about it. I was quiet but couldn't stop thinking about the type of media-born delusion I just saw.

The Kids in Cages BS and Call for Open Borders.

The funniest part of this BS was Rachel Maddow fake crying. So when illegals with children cross the border, there are many issues: they get separated because our country doesn't jail a bunch of children with adults; we have no idea who these people are; and these children might not even be the kids of these adults. It all started with a report on Twitter that kids were being put in cages (processing centers where they were held a week or two at max) under the Trump administration. The only problem was that the reporter was using a picture from 2014, which was during Obama's era. Kids who were sleeping in tin foil blankets in cages waiting to be processed under the Obama administration were used in pictures to say that Trump was a horrible monster.

Of course the media collectively didn't say much about this mess-up with the pictures and they quickly ran with the story and pretended like nothing happened. So then all the crazy brainwashed liberals, professional protestors, celebs with a need to get back on the radar, and Dem senators up for reelection rushed to the border to get in front of cameras and to see who could cry on cue better. My pick for this was a dem senator from Oregon who was so fake, moronic, and funny, all wrapped into one. Then of course there was Rachel Maddow who was on her show at MSNBC, and she tried to fake hold herself back from crying too. She bent over in her chair pretending not to let the cameras see her fake balling her eyes out. She tried to fake send it off to another reporter while she pretended to bend over and cried. *It was hilarious!*

Thousands of protesters held corny signs that read, "Children belong with their families" and "He's not my president!" *So funny! So hilarious!* Telemundo television set up a cage that was about four feet tall, put a kid in the cage, told him to cry, and took close-up pictures of him. They sent it all around the world. Many brainwashed Democrats thought this was real, because why would the media lie, right? The brainwashed zombies posted it all over their Facebook and pretended to be outraged for likes, and attention. Anyone who dared to tell them the truth by showing the wide shot of the pictures that were leaked were met with hysteria and outrage. No one was allowed to tell anyone the truth. Whatever the media said was real, and how dare you say otherwise. These were scary times.

But then of course was the famous image of the little girl being separated from her mother at the border, with the audio of the little girl crying, that was used over and over everywhere. Later we would find out about the mother's financial situation in Mexico; she was not in need at all of coming to America. Someone did a price analysis on her little girls' clothes, from the images being used all over the internet, and the little girl was wearing expensive kid jeans, boots, and shirt. This was a middle-class Mexican citizen crossing the border with her daughter to make more money in America.

I decided to see how my Hispanic friends were doing and what effect the propaganda had on them, if any. Surely, they were over our fight about made-up liberal shit like white privilege. It was Friday night so I figured everyone would be drinking tequila, smoking weed, and having fun. I walked into their house in Pomona and saw Juan, Manuel, Juan's girlfriend, and some other Hispanic acquaintances I've known throughout the years, and they were all crying. They were all huddled around the kitchen table, listening to the little girl, who had better jeans on than I did, balling. The little girl's mother broke the law and was being punished for it, and now it was America's fault. As soon as I walked in everyone looked at me. Juan stood up straight, pointed his finger at me and said, "I can't believe you support Donald Trump now!"

The whole room full of Hispanic friends and acquaintances, some of them anchor babies, illegal, or third and fourth generation Mexican-American citizens, looked at me and gasped. I just stood there not knowing what to say. I had my arms out and my chin scrunched up to my chest. "I brought Tequila," I said. The next three hours was everyone sitting around the kitchen table, drinking tequila, Modelo, eating tamales, and arguing about Donald Trump. "Juan, we can't let the whole world come here; if we let the whole world come here, no one will have any jobs," I told him."

"No, you white people won't have any jobs!" he proclaimed.

"Maybe. Which would be a problem for about 70% of the population," I explained.

"Not a problem for me!" he stated.

"So all white people should be homeless then?" I asked.

"That's fine, you stole this land from Mexico," he told me.

"Actually no it was the Indians' land first, then the Spanish, but it's both of ours now," I told him.

"It doesn't matter!" he said, which was what he said when faced with any facts he didn't like. I sighed.

"Ok, Juan, so there's a hundred and eighty million people in Mexico; let's say we have open borders. What happens when the populations from Honduras, Brazil, Colombia, and Argentina come? We just went from a population of 300 million people to 600 million people. Where are these people going to stay and where are these people going to work?" I asked, as I couldn't believe that this was even an argument that needed to be had with a major political party of the United States.

"That's not my problem!" he stated. I sighed again in disbelief.

"It *will* be your problem when they are sitting on your lawn looking for food," I told him. This is the way the conversation went for hours. He wanted open borders, because of some kind of connection to people he never met, and any negative consequences to it was not *his* problem. *It was hopeless to try to make him see the light.* I knew he'd have to get it eventually or be run over by hungry illegal immigrants from Honduras. Over the next few weeks I hung out with Juan more and more. As we talked, he began to understand, or at least pretended to shut me up. He had a good job, a good salary, and a lot of freedom in America. All of that would be gone with open borders, and once he got past the emotions of it, he was reasonable and understanding again. It took time for him to see the truth like it did for me, but as the craziness continued, eventually and surprisingly he would no longer consider himself a Democrat.

And Then the Most Uncomfortable Thing Happened.

Augusta came over. He smiled and shook my hand. We pretended like our argument about how he was oppressed by white privilege never happened. We talked about the Lakers and about his new restaurant; it was like everything was the way it used to be.

He told me about a fight he got into with a Hispanic *cholo* at a Mexican salsa club. He snickered, "Hey I'm not racist, but if I was, I'd be on your side."

He then laughed and said it was a joke, but it wasn't funny. It wasn't racist to build a wall to stop illegal immigration or to stop any immigration at all. Almost everything the media called racist wasn't. But how do you tell someone they are being manipulated, and their skin color is being used like a pawn in a sick game for power and control.

Instead of letting it pass, I sighed, placed my hand on his shoulder, and with complete sincerity said, "I don't want you to think that I'm racist. I'm not."

Augusta smirked, picked up my bottle of tequila, and took a swig of it. It was like no matter what any white person ever told him, he'd always be suspicious. I was beginning to feel the same way. Any person with skin a shade darker than milk, I would wonder if they secretly resented me for something I didn't do two hundred years ago. The term racist had been used and abused so much by the Democrats and their friends in the media over the past few years that, as it were now, everything could be considered racist.

Augusta went on to talk about something else. As he continued to talk and I continued to listen, I couldn't help but to think about how confusing it must be to be Black in America right now.

Black people had white liberals telling them that everything under the sun was racist and that white people were out to get them if they didn't vote Democrat. Then the liberal mainstream media cherry-picked stories of police brutality, twisting most of the facts, while leaving out other information to fit the narrative that the system was rigged against them. Over the last few years, they were also being told that white people had everything handed to them, wherever they went. White privilege was like that Eddie Murphy skit where he walked around with makeup on that made him look white, and people handed him money. It used to be an SNL skit that people laughed at, but now it was supposed to be taken seriously or it meant you were racist. Black people were told that big government would help them, when, really, it had only ever hurt them. Black people were told that they *had* to be Democrats, even though Democrats had done nothing but scare them into thinking that everyone was racist.

As I listened to Augusta speak, I realized that if I were Black, I wouldn't know what to believe either. Who could you trust and how would you know for sure what was going on? Black conservatives like Candace Owens, Thomas Sowell, Larry Elder, and Ben Carson were anomalies and relatively hard to find for the average person—people who thought for themselves, and who found the truth, but were silenced by the mainstream media. Kanye West was a very bad problem for the mainstream liberal media. He was a huge superstar that they now decided to hate and ignore.

This was such a confusing time for everyone, and probably even more confusing if you are Black. Hell, they had me thinking everything could be free my whole life. They had me thinking that the person at the local auto parts store was oppressed because he had to work for a living. They had me thinking that hard work was oppression. They had me thinking that America was oppressive because people had to make a living for themselves. They had me thinking that socialism was the answer to everyone's problems. It's so bizarre now when I think about it.

Donald Trump was a giant reset button for America. Maybe Augusta would one day have an *aha!* moment like I did and realize he was being misled. Or maybe Augusta would live his entire life always thinking America was out to get him because of his skin color. The hardest part was knowing I couldn't help him.

What Felt Like My First 4th of July, in a California I No Longer Knew.

My Fourth of July started early in the morning when I was checking my Facebook, and one of those little memory posts popped up. It was a memory of my Fourth of July two years ago, and low and behold it was a picture I posted of another American Indian. I looked at it and was again disgusted with myself. This Facebook memory was from July 2016, and at that time I was so disappointed that Bernie Sanders didn't get the nomination. Two years later, after learning what a fucking lunatic Bernie Sanders and all the rest of the Democrats were, I was thrilled Donald Trump was president. However, California was not.

From protests and illogical thinking all across America, we had the liberal capital California attempt to ban the Bible, and straws (yes, straws). They had come out in favor of paying for illegal immigrant healthcare, sanctuary cities, and a tax on gas because it would be a great way to save the environment. My two favorites of the year from California were decriminalizing giving someone AIDS and making it a six-month jail sentence for misgendering someone. California had become like a screaming child, not capable of understanding what was going on when Trump became president. So I went into the primaries of the midterm elections and voted Republican for the first time in my life.

I walked into the polling place being the only white person in the room. Everyone looked at me and it felt like everyone instinctively knew what I was there to do. When I voted I heard two tiny Latina girls in the booth next to me speak in Spanish. The only English thing I could hear was Trump. I knew what they were there to do. I doubted the men who signed the Declaration of Independence on July 4, 1776, would have ever imagined this. I realized that the 4th of July had been a day I took for granted. Now it seemed to have a different—bittersweet—meaning. Brian and I were drinking at a bar right off the beach in Belmont Shore, where sailboats were out on the ocean. I looked out and wondered how I could ever be angry at a beautiful country like this. "I'm moving back to Indiana," Brian said. I was shocked and dropped my drink down on the table and it spilled. The bartender came over and helped me clean it up.

"What?! Why?" I asked loudly, confused.

"I'm moving back," Brian said matter-of-factly. "What do you mean why? Are you serious?"

"No, I know but...at least wait till November. Wait till the midterms to see what happens," I said.

Brian smirked and laughed, "Yeah I know what's going to happen." I looked at him perturbed almost like the liberal I once was.

"California is going red! There's no way people will vote for this stuff!" I said.

Brian smiled more and shook his head, "No man, they will."

I looked at him in disbelief. "You don't see it?! This stuff is crazy! California won't vote for this!" I said loudly.

"This stuff *is* crazy, and California is just crazy enough to vote for it," he said. I helped the bartender wipe up my drink as best I could with napkins.

"Yeah, but...you'll see...it's going red in November—it has to. You'll see and you will be sad you left when all this shit gets turned around," I told him confidently.

Brian smirked some more, "Yeah, I hope you're right, for your sake." Brian looked at me seriously, knowing I might never leave California; he also knew what it would potentially mean for me if it never did get turned around. The popping of fireworks began. I followed Brian and the rest of the bar out to the deck where the fireworks lit up the sky, as boats traveled across the sea. I thought to myself, *No matter what happened, now that I know the truth, I'm going to be okay. California would surely go red, and America would begin to wake up from this nonsense like I had.* I stood there holding my drink and closed my eyes as fireworks lit up my face, and I prayed for the first time since 2008. I did it for the same reason I did then, which was change. However, this time, I didn't do it hoping America would change; I did it hoping people would look within themselves like I had and change.

My Sister Janet and Kanye West

This was my sister's newfound nemesis on the internet. The reason for this was because Kanye West was evidence that everything she believed her whole life was false, just like I had. After waking up to the truth I began to notice the same trend with all liberals. They clung to one or many narratives all at once, none based on fact, only on feelings; it was just as Possum Mike McDowell and Ben Shapiro said. These feelings came from the TV, internet, music, or news, which were all entirely controlled by a boomer hippie liberal viewpoint. Our culture had so many strange narratives stemming from the sixties revolution. Many of them had begun to fade away for me.

My sister Janet believed in the white versus black ideology for years, and I believed in the poor versus rich ideology. Her ideology was that the whole white world was out to get Black people, and everything bad in Black people's lives was the result of white people, racism, or slavery. My ideology was the same except the poor were oppressed and the rich were the oppressors. Both were ideologies and not facts, however it was her ideology that cranked up during the Obama years with Black Lives Matter. It eventually took over the original Marxist ideology that was poor versus rich in our culture.

The reason for that seemed pretty obvious to me when I began to look at the statistics of immigration, and the use of the phrase "people of color." Democrats had found their "in" to get the kind of "hope and change" they wanted, and their decision was made. When Kanye West wore the MAGA hat, not just once but everywhere, it was reality ripping up Janet's Democrat media-shaped worldview. There were multiple kinds of narratives being exposed with liberals every day, hence the outrage and hatred for Donald Trump. Donald Trump's rational Americans told liberals that they were not oppressed and that they were entitled to nothing, 24 hours a day, 7 days a week. Donald Trump was figuratively telling liberals that their perception was not reality. And sometimes Donald Trump even taunted them by tweeting about it.

Kanye West was my darkly tanned Afro hair-wearing sister's red pill, which she was fighting like hell not to take. She was constantly posting how much she hated him all over Facebook. It was hilarious!

But also sad and disturbing at the same time. She despised this guy, all because he told the world that the word racist was not going to control him and that he was free and not oppressed by anyone. But she couldn't let it go; Black people *had* to be oppressed, because Don Lemon and the rest of the Democrat media told her so. How would they continue to win elections without winning the inner city states, by putting fear into Black people that white people were racist? It was what Janet's whole life was built on. It's what gave her life meaning. If Black people were *not* oppressed, what would there be for her to fight for and worry about?

I had been going over a similar question of my own. If capitalism was *not* evil, and America's corporations and CEOs were *not* oppressing people, what was I to fight for? My whole adult life, I had always thought I knew of a better way. My whole career in film and books, I thought I had to make the world a better place. I even turned down projects from friends into which I couldn't insert my socialist ideologies. Capitalism wasn't bad; it was great, because it's how I have the life I do. It's not a perfect life, but it's my life, and I chose it. Thinking about all those years I resented America and capitalism, it all seemed so stupid and ridiculous. It was like the weight of the world had been lifted off of my shoulders. Maybe the boomer hippie movement of the sixties was a rejection of the responsibilities that was handed down to them from their parents. Or maybe it was just the beginning of a diabolical plan to destroy America from within.

All I knew was that my sister and I were descendants of it, and I was witnessing her go through the hardest part, which was accepting that her worldview wasn't reality. Her worldview was a carefully crafted and shaped image, just like mine was. As she was posting on Facebook, her usual hate for Kanye West, just as I once did with capitalism or corporations, Janet was all but calling Kanye West the N word when I stupidly tried to explain to her that he was *not* crazy like the media said he was. As I would have done myself if someone explained to me that America and capitalism wasn't oppressive, and my worldview wasn't correct, she went out bombs blasting, and at one point even called me a cocksucker.

She furiously typed out her resume to show me how qualified she was, to know that the KKK was around every corner. I figured that telling her that there were only 3,000 KKK members in America, which was less than 0.1 percent of our population, might cause her to have an aneurysm, so I decided against it. However I held out hope that she would reevaluate her beliefs when the Democrats did not win both the senate and house, which would be only the fourth time in history. Trump was right when he said he wanted to Make America Great Again. I had no idea what that meant until I saw what was wrong within myself and in my psychologically subverted sister.

The Caravan, My First Trump Rally, and the Midterms.

We started to see this caravan forming of people who were coming from South America who were all headed to our southern border. It formed to be about ten thousand people. If you turned on CNN, they would tell you to believe that this caravan formed organically, before the midterms. Mexico surprisingly said that they would not let them pass, however the caravan of people broke through their fences and their police barriers, and they stormed through Mexico's border with the Mexican government pretty much giving them directions on which way to go. It was unreal to see, and the media acted like it was no big deal, and that if there was anyone concerned with this, they were racist or crazy. It was similar to what they said about the white farmers getting killed by Black south Africans for land earlier in the summer. Every dead white farmer was a white supremacy conspiracy theory, so keep quiet, racist!

The narrative was that we should all just welcome these people breaking through countries with open arms, because we are a nation of immigrants they said. I knew with my new sources of information that this was a lie. We were not a nation of immigrants; we were a nation of citizens with laws. We had only let immigrants from nonwhite countries into the United States since 1965. If CNN and this progressive swath of activist journalists wanted to keep immigration going, maybe they should stop telling immigrants that white men have privilege and are bad. It was clear CNN and liberals had an agenda. They cared more about the rest of the world than they did their own citizens, all because half of the country knew math, voted for lower taxes, and had white skin.

Obama was the first outgoing president to ever campaign against his succeeding president in the midterms, and he acted as if this caravan of ten thousand people looking to cross the border was nothing to worry about too. The momentum was building as this caravan got closer, and it wasn't looking good for the people of virtue, and you could see it on their faces. Rational people don't side with ten thousand strangers from another country who want to illegally enter. I'm almost positive that has never happened in the history of the world. Liberals were no longer rational, but even some of them were flinching.

Then suddenly, the caravan slowed down. Just like that. What was supposed to magically appear at our border on November 6, 2018, which was voting day, was no longer moving. It seemed as if a rich liberal billionaire (cough, George Soros, cough) thought this was a winning issue, and quickly learned it wasn't. We had already known that they were being fed, given water, and given buses and trucks to make their way through Mexico. It was clear that this caravan of ten thousand people with food, water, and transportation, took an extreme amount of coordination and planning.

The liberal propaganda machine seemed like it didn't want anyone to know that though. None of these people were journalists anymore. None of them did their jobs as journalists, which was to find out the truth. They were more like cheerleaders of the progressive communist Democratic Party. I didn't know if it was just extreme bias or some diabolical conspiracy that had been progressing for years. The only thing I knew was that I was happy that a man who was grounded and never influenced by emotional hysterical liberalism, like I once was, was our president.

I never would have imagined in 2016, when I couldn't sleep because Trump was president, that I'd ever be as happy as I was now. I wanted to meet the man who changed my life and changing millions of lives. When I learned Donald Trump was going to be at a rally in Las Vegas, I knew I had to make the five-hour drive from Los Angeles. I drove my hybrid up the 215 freeway. As I drove, I thought about the last time I drove this freeway to Vegas, and how angry I was when Bernie Sanders lost the primary. I never would have guessed I'd be a registered Republican two years later. *Now the whole thing just seemed so silly.* Did I really think I was oppressed because my car battery was dead two years ago? Did I really yell at a bartender because she wanted me to pay for something to use the bathroom? The economy was soaring under Trump better than it had in fifty years. Did I really think the world was coming to an end because of capitalism? Did I really think the economy was going to collapse under Trump and thrive under Bernie Sanders' socialism? What was wrong with me two years ago? It was like I was in some kind of illogical haze the whole time Obama was president. It was like I was in some kind of haze most of my life.

I thought that maybe if California doesn't go red I would move to a red state one day like my friend Brian did, like when he went back to Indiana. *Maybe I'd move to Montana.* I arrived at Vegas two hours before the Trump rally, and right away I saw a line of people two blocks long. I couldn't believe it. Police had to close off an entire neighborhood. *Damn! I was so stupid.* Of course I wasn't going to get into a Trump rally showing up only two hours early. What would you expect from the greatest president in the last sixty years? I was terribly disappointed that I wouldn't be able to see the man that had such a profound impact on my life. I knew I wasn't going to see the commander and chief, so I did the only rational thing any freedom loving American would do, I stopped off at a nearby KFC to order a bucket of chicken. But that's when something phenomenal happened.

It was something so unbelievable that it had to be ordained by fate. I'm inside KFC and in line ordering, when I saw a black secret service car with government plates pull into the parking lot and stop. I was waiting for my food as I see these two secret service men come in, and stand in line across from me. I'm standing there, looking at them, and looking at their car outside, in disbelief. I'm thinking to myself, *No way is this possible right now.* The two secret service men saw me staring at them like a freak, so I decided to just come out with it already, so that I wouldn't scare them. "Hey, are you the president's guys or something?!" I asked. They both had dark sunglasses on.

The one closest to me said, "We can't give you any information on that." I quickly pretended to act normal.

"Oh well, I was trying to get into the Trump rally, but it's all closed off," I said. The one closest to me looks me up and down. "I can tell you might be a supporter of his. If you are, I might be able to tell him something for you." *Oh, wow!* The excitement I felt began to crawl all over me.

"You could?!" I ask excitedly.

"Sure, why not?" the secret service agent said. My eyes widened with bewilderment as I began to think. The thought of the President of the United States knowing that I support him, almost brought a tear to my eye. But then in an instant, I knew exactly what I want him to tell the greatest president of my lifetime.

"Could you tell him he changed my life?!" I asked. The KFC cashier was looking at me, wondering what the hell I was talking about. But I was so excited that I could barely contain myself. The Secret Service guy looked a bit shocked.

"Sure, I could tell him that. What's your name?" he asked as he pulled out a pen and paper from his coat pocket. My arms flapped together hitting the sides of myself like a penguin, as I continued to get happier.

"My name?!.... My name is Roman! I'm from Indiana, and I'm free! I'm free and I love America!" I said as I smacked my hand down on the counter, then shook my fists in the air. I grabbed my bucket of chicken from the stunned cashier and strolled out of the KFC. After that, I had no regrets about the five-hour drive back.

March 23, 2019, the Fake News is Exposed with the End of the Russian Collusion Delusion.

It had been four months and a lot of the crazy rhetoric had died down. Maybe people were finally telling Democrats to shut up. Or maybe they were fatigued by all the outrage. Trump had won the Senate but lost the house in November. This was the first time in a hundred years the incoming president didn't lose both. A lot of the anti-white rhetoric also died down, thank God; but there seemed to be a new target for them to blame everything on, which was Jews. They had come full circle and were now the very thing they hated the most, which was the Alt-Right. However the progressive-socialist-left had things far more familiar with the Alt-Right than anyone could have imagined. The Democrats voted in a socialist named Alexandria Ocasio-Cortez and two Muslim socialists named Illhan Omar and Rashida Talib. All three supported Palestine and were against Israel's existence altogether.

There were other very strange socialist characters from the Democratic Party, all throughout the government, from one place to the next. However these new socialist women who hated Jews, white people, capitalism, and America really stood out. Just hearing all these new house of representative members speak was a redpill all on its own. They said one crazy thing after another, and the likeminded far left socialist media went ballistic for it. They loved them. They were on every late-night TV show; it was as if they were heroes who just saved earth. I on the other hand had been in the process of deprogramming myself the past year, and listening to how far gone Alexandria Ocasio-Cortez was, sure helped. I thanked god that I was no longer as brainwashed as she was. Ironically, she's a millennial who loves Bernie Sanders too. She believed the world will come to an end in twelve years from global warming if we don't ban cars and airplanes. You never know, aliens could come down and give us all environmentally friendly spaceships too. *It was getting that strange.* Miss Cortez also believed, like the rest of the Democratic Party, that Donald Trump is a Russian spy.

If you remember, I was thrown off of a film set for daring to say otherwise. March 23, 2019 was the end of the Mueller report, after two years of investigation. Robert Mueller found no collusion by Donald Trump with Russia, and the Department of Justice found no obstruction. The media talked about this story for two years straight. The media had political analyst after political analyst for two years straight who insinuated that Donald Trump was a Russian spy, who was being manipulated by Vladimir Putin. So what happened when Robert Mueller found no collusion? For one, Rachel Maddow cried again. Her whole career was pretty much banking on this nonsense. She even ran a story once that said the Russians might turn off our electricity in the winter to freeze us all to death. This was all Trump's evil conservative plan of course. This was journalism in 2019, three years after Trump was elected.

I decided to buzz my hair. With all the ridiculous media narratives out of my head, I wanted the hair on top gone as well. So I got my hair buzzed short. I took my girlfriend out to Hollywood for drinks and dinner. I wore a shirt I bought online that said, "Conservatism Is the New Punk Rock" under my suit jacket. *Holy shit, that's the truth!* I said to myself when I first saw it. As we were walking down the sidewalk in Hollywood, my girlfriend stopped me by grabbing my arm. "Baby look!" she said. I looked down and was standing on Donald Trump's Star on the Hollywood Walk of Fame.

"Oh shit! Take a picture of me!" I said. My girlfriend took my phone and snapped a picture; and of course she wanted one too, so I took one of her as well. Donald Trump was now an American legend. The Mueller report proving no Russian collusion and no obstruction collapsed the biggest hoax perpetrated on the American people ever. It was the death punch of the liberal mainstream media machine. It was the death punch of liberalism and all of its bogus narratives and pseudosciences since the 1960s. Forever people will always know that liberal News is fake news, has an agenda, and a worldview that it's trying to instill in you. People will always know that Donald Trump had been right all along, and that the mainstream liberal media *is* the enemy of the people.

It was the same media that made me believe George W. Bush was Hitler while I was in college. It was the same media that told me as a young impressionable adult, when I was at my most vulnerable moment during the recession, that capitalism didn't work anymore. It was the same media that told me socialism was the answer to everyone's problems, including my own. It was the same media that told me to hate America, because of its history. It was the same media that tried to get my friends to hate me for being white. On March 23,

2019, social media in Los Angeles, was in complete silence. You could hear a pin drop. No one said anything—maybe out of fear, or maybe out of shock. There were now many more people just like me, dealing with the same thing I just went through the past year. Their worldviews had exploded in their faces. I texted all three of my friends who kicked me off of that film set that day. They were all 100% sure Trump was a Russian spy, even though it had been exposed as a lie by Project Veritas. Now that the lie had been exposed *again* and by the person doing the investigating, I texted all of them. Not even one of them responded. Maybe they were holding onto hope that Mueller was a Russian spy too, which was the media's new narrative. Or maybe they were filled with hate for me, because I dared to question their liberal overlords.

Or maybe they were busy crying in a car, twenty miles outside of San Diego like I did, when I came to the realization that everything I had been told my entire life was a lie. The Mueller report had redpilled generations of more people—I was almost positive of it. Luckily for me, I was about a year ahead. The hard part was over. However the fight for freeing people from their mental prisons was *not* over by a long shot. Hong and I walked down the Hollywood sidewalk to a Chinese restaurant where we decided to get dinner. In the alley of the restaurant, on the white brick wall, we both saw red spray paint that said "Fuck white people."

Somehow I don't think this is what Martin Luther King Jr. envisioned in his "I Have a Dream" speech. Hong, disgusted with the sight, said, "Stupid people! Their brain sick!" I looked at the spray paint, and felt indifferent for the poor soul stuck in the liberal propaganda machine.

"Have you ever thought about moving to Montana?" I asked.

"Montan-a?! So cold, baby!" Hong stated. We continued to walk to the front door of the restaurant.

"Yeah you're right. It might be more fun to stick around Los Angeles to piss people off," I said with a smile on my face. I was free from the thoughts that once shaped the world around me, and the future had endless possibilities. This was a gift that I couldn't ever possibly pay back. But what I can do is vote Trump 2020.